EXCLUSIVE

Reporters in Love . . . and War

I arrived in the Gloomroom so early the next morning even Jim Mulvaney was at peace. The boy wonder sat quietly, drinking coffee he did not spill.

At my own desk, a few rows away, I opened the newspaper to my story on page five. Nice. The best stories of the day ran "upfront," on pages three through seven. If your story ran there it meant you'd "got good play." Everyone said it like that, as if it was a sexual act. As a tryout, I couldn't have gotten better play.

I read my story, sitting sideways. Without moving my head, I shifted my eyes back, far as I could. He was still there. I turned again to the front page and sighed to signal that good play bored me. I got good play often.

He stood, walked over quickly. Slowly, he held out his hand.

"Hullo, I'm Jim Mulvaney." He smiled, but not with his mouth.

He looked down at my legs and quickly up again. His blue eyes seared.

They also steamed, accused, and sent troops to fight an ill-advised war.

"Go away," I said.

"You always so good at making friends?" He examined me as if he were trying to imagine if I could be interested in him.

I examined him back, trying to figure out if this was an act.

He was dressed for a stakeout: cop shoes, another dreadful plaid shirt, coffee stain in place.

"We've already met," I said.

"I don't think so."

So he had shoved me and did not remember. This Mulvaney wasn't merely a deranged Irishman. He was a deranged, *self-absorbed* Irishman.

"Barbara Fischkin," I said, knowing I shouldn't.

EXCL

Barbara Fischkin

Reporters in Love . . . and War

USIVE

A NOVEL

DELTA TRADE PAPERBACKS

EXCLUSIVE
REPORTERS IN LOVE . . . AND WAR: A NOVEL
A Delta Trade Paperback / June 2005

Published by
Bantam Dell
A Division of Random House, Inc.
New York, New York

The first five stanzas of "The Ballad of the Tinker's Wife" from *Ballads of a Bogman*
by Sigerson Clifford. Copyright © 1986 by the Estate of Sigerson Clifford.
Reprinted by kind permission of Mercier Press Ltd., Cork, Ireland.

Book design by Glen M. Edelstein

Delta is a registered trademark of Random House, Inc.,
and the colophon is a trademark of Random House, Inc.

Library of Congress Cataloging in Publication Data
Fischkin, Barbara.
Exclusive : reporters in love—and war : a novel / Barbara Fischkin.
p. cm.
ISBN 038533799X
1. Journalists—Fiction.   2. Jewish women—Fiction.   3. Irish Americans—Fiction.
4. Americans—Foreign countries—Fiction.   5. New York (N.Y.)—Fiction.
6. Adventure fiction.   7. Love stories.
PS3606.I768 E97 2005
813/.6 22
2005041447

Printed in the United States of America
Published simultaneously in Canada

www.bantamdell.com

BVG   10 9 8 7 6 5 4 3 2 1

For Dan and Jack,
our kids

This book is based, casually, on our lives.
Some of it is even true.

EXCLUSIVE

My husband, Jim Mulvaney, dashing and handsome though he may be, is delusional about his appeal to the human race. Let me walk you inside his brain: It is a Saturday in America. Summer. Inside Mulvaney's brain, it is always summer. No school, no shoes, no shirts. Not even his favorite shirts, plaid with coffee stains. On this sunlit day, men are mowing lawns, pitching baseballs to their sons, having sex with their wives. Suddenly, all these Viagra-free specimens, all these fathers of exclusively male children, have a single thought.

They all want to go to the movies.

And why is that?

The Jim Mulvaney Story.

"Mulvaney!" I say. "You have to be kidding."

He isn't.

"Their wives will love it, too," he tells me.

His blue eyes flash like a smile; that is never a good sign. My middle-aged, long-term husband still believes that every one of his stories is a gem. Even the ones he makes up. As in: Is that "true-true" or "Mulvaney-true"?

Some of his stories *are* gems.

He was, for example, the last white guy out of Tiananmen Square.

That's a true-true story, packed with danger and suspense. Unless you've heard it twenty, thirty times.

I have.

Now, when those eyes of his gleam and he starts using the

little Mandarin he knows, I fake a paper cut, an asthma attack, a hemorrhage if need be.

But let's get back to the movie.

"Mulvaney," I say, "I just can't see people rushing off in droves to see a movie about a middle-class kid from Queens who became a newspaper reporter."

This is when he reminds me that he wasn't *just* a newspaper reporter.

"I was a *foreign correspondent,*" he says, affecting the professorial tone he developed at forty.

"So were half your friends, Mulvaney. You don't see them foaming at the mouth to tell their life stories."

He swaggers up to his certificate.

"I know," I say. "You won a Pulitzer Prize. So did three-quarters of your friends."

"Barbara," he says, "need I remind you that I was the last white guy out of Tiananmen Square?"

No matter where he works, my husband will always be the quintessential newspaper reporter. He understands the criminal mind, the tortured psyche of the downtrodden. So why does he have such a hard time figuring out himself? He can't, for example, imagine why he isn't rich. It's not, he says, as if he doesn't try. Over the years, he has proposed any number of get-rich-quick schemes, including the manufacture of one-size-fits-all dentures. "I need you in on this" is what he always tells me. "Mulvaney," I say, "I am a writer, not a dental hygienist." If I have one job as a wife, it is to dissuade Mulvaney. He says we would be rich if I helped him. I say we would be rich if he had a longer attention span.

"We'll need a book to go with the movie," he says.

I want to be my husband's biographer about as badly as I want to open a restaurant that serves fried bugs (another can't-lose "moneymaker," based on a Mexican concept that would not have traveled well).

"You've got it backward," I say, hoping to distract him. "Books come first, or at least they should."

"You have to write the book," he says. "You are a writer and you know me better than anyone in the world."

Often, I wish I didn't.

"Maybe we both can write the movie and the book," he says. "We can write together."

I remind him we do very little together without having an argument. Taking out the garbage requires an arms negotiator and a peace accord. The word that comes to most people's minds when they describe us is "incompatible."

Even my mother agreed that Mulvaney and I were incompatible, although she did not see this as a problem.

"Marriage, dear, is not about daily comforts," she told me. "It's not about getting along and it's certainly not related to anyone's career."

Who, I asked her, said anything about marriage? "Who said anything about marrying *Mulvaney*?"

"Marriage," my mother insisted, "is about whether you can tell funny stories, even in hard times, preferably about one another."

She believed we could, perhaps should, invent those stories. Like Mulvaney, my mother is not a stickler for veracity.

ACT ONE

CHAPTER 1

The Barbara Fischkin Story

On a muggy summer morning in the early eighties, I crept along in my war-torn Chevy Nova, inching east with the station wagons on the packed Long Island Expressway. The sign at the construction site said to merge. Fiddling for a city radio station without static, yearning for anything decent, I almost missed my allotted opportunity to squeeze into the only open lane, causing the man behind me to honk wildly, as if this tie-up was all my fault. But crankiness does not cause traffic. It is the other way around. A lone seagull fluttered through the carbon monoxide, and on WBAB, Radio Long Island, disco blared. I couldn't believe they still played disco here. Hadn't John Travolta just checked into a nursing home?

Why, I asked myself, was I on my way to the Suffolk County bureau of *Newsday*? Why was I even on Long Island, a place I swore I would never live or work?

Because I wanted a better job, if not *in* Manhattan, at least close to it.

But was it worth *this*?

I had to remind myself of the facts.

I worked at the *Knickerbocker News,* a small afternoon daily in Albany, a paper that viewed winning the Pulitzer Prize as a vicarious experience. *Newsday,* I told myself, might not be the *New York Times*. But unlike the *Times,* it had the good taste to do more with my résumé than throw it out.

And unlike the paltry *"Knick,"* *Newsday* had a circulation of 600,000 and growing. So what if it called itself "America's Finest Suburban Newspaper"? At least its slogan wasn't "You've got to get *The Knick* at Night." I'd been in Albany long enough. Gone to college there, too, a misdirected journey that began because I didn't want to live with my parents in Brooklyn. Brooklyn wasn't Manhattan.

Miraculously, another lane opened. I enjoyed an entire five seconds of carefree driving before another seagull, a bigger one, landed on the road in front of my car. Why didn't these birds stay at the beach where they belonged? I slammed on the brakes and, as the human honking behind me accelerated, swerved and saved that stupid gull's life. In celebration, I flicked off the radio. Even if I could dance, I would have hated disco music. Its philosophy, though, was another matter: Twirl fast, long, and hard with a *temporary* partner. I had nothing against romance, even a quasi-exclusive romance, as long as it didn't get in the way of my job or my own adventures.

Like the men in Albany did.

The men in Albany, the ones I wound up with anyway, were all Irish and certifiable. Sure, they looked presentable on the surface, even good-looking, thanks to several generations of American nutrition. But they were the types who would invite you cross-country skiing, then get you lost for hours on a trail that headed nowhere, including home. Albany, I was convinced, was where Irish Catholic boys—they were all Catholic—went after they robbed stagecoaches or tied up their mothers but before they were sent permanently to hell. It was like that island where Pinocchio grew donkey ears, except in Albany bad boys were admitted into the Ancient Order of Hibernians.

The sanest man I knew in Albany was, unfortunately, Mario Cuomo. Irish, no. Catholic, yes. Cuomo was about to become governor and the party faithful believed that eventually he would be President, because he was such a great orator and an intellect, too.

Usually, all Mario Cuomo ever said to *me* was "Barbara! You've lost weight."

I was not as flattered as he'd assumed I'd be. But it did convince me that Mario Cuomo was, indeed, brilliant. When he made that remark, phrasing it as a statement and not as a question, it always made me stop and remember the way my mother would scream gleefully, at the top of her lungs from a dressing room in the Juniors department of Macy's Flatbush Avenue:

"That is not a dress for you! That is a dress for some flat-chested little Twiggy!"

Sometimes I'd forget the question I wanted to ask him.

Also, Mario Cuomo was married, apparently monogamous, and too old, although not as old as some of the people I covered. As the junior reporter in the Capitol Bureau, one of my assignments was the dreaded "After Sixty" column. Since I myself was solidly Under Thirty, the *Knick News* refused to run my photograph with it.

In retaliation—and to combat boredom—I decided that the "senior" beat needed a criminal justice angle. Within a year, I'd interviewed all the old people in state prisons, always asking Cuomo for comment.

"Lieutenant Governor, don't you think this man has served his time?"

"Barbara," he'd reply, *"you look thin."*

Newsday had to be better.

Only I didn't have a job there yet.

All they'd said was that I could "try out" for a week. They were going to make me *prove* that I could cover Long Island, and I couldn't even perform this humiliating audition in a civilized atmosphere.

Newsday's headquarters were on Stewart Avenue in the rarefied village of Garden City, in the heart of Nassau County, a mere twenty-six minutes from Times Square. But I had been told to go to the Suffolk County bureau instead. It was in a place I'd never heard mentioned in any book or movie: Ronkonkoma, New York.

I saw a bumper sticker that said *Pray for Me. I Ride the L.I.E.* In front of me stretched more cars, more road. On my right and left I passed the backs of housing developments and shopping centers. I didn't think I would like Long Island any better from the front.

Particularly not Ronkonkoma.

Ronkonkoma was smack in the middle of Suffolk County, and Suffolk County, according to my quick research, was the second of Long Island's two counties, the stepsister, the wild, wild east until you got to the Hamptons. I already knew as much about Long Island as I wanted, and it was my impression that the Hamptons didn't count as part of it, inhabited as they were by summer people who read only the *Times* and believed they were in Martha's Vineyard.

No, the Hamptons had nothing to do with Ronkonkoma. Ronkonkoma was very far and yet not far enough.

The traffic became worse. At L.I.E. Exit 60, late for the first newspaper audition of my life, I negotiated the relentless curve of an off-ramp and decided that those who passed into the heart of Suffolk County never returned. The cars I saw traveling west were a mirage.

Off the expressway, I got lost.

Most of the houses had aluminum siding. Wood and brick appeared sparingly, as if those materials were proscribed under some odd suburban rationing program. On the relentless commercial strips, I calculated one pizzeria and two fast-food emporiums for every ten aluminum-sided houses. For variety there was a fried clams and ice cream stand with a plastic orange roof. And for gourmets, a Ground Round.

Maybe *Newsday* would see it my way and move its Suffolk bureau out to the Hamptons, the *chic* Long Island, if you could imagine such a thing.

Then I could fly to work.

In a private jet.

Mulvaney is looking over my shoulder.

"The book is supposed to be about me! Why is Mario Cuomo in it?"

I have not actually agreed to write anything.

"Well, you knew Cuomo, too...."

"But you don't talk about me and Mario," he says, pointing like a madman to the delete key. "This is about *you* and Mario! You are not supposed to provide excruciating, irrelevant information about your early life unless you are a really famous author. Which you will be. Once you write about me."

"Mulvaney," I inform him, "if I do write a book about you, it will be mostly about me."

"Okay, so you want to include your childhood because you were already dreaming about me then. You were in love with me before you even met me."

I have to admit there is a sweetness to his strategy that disarms me. He can still do that, so I do not say what I am thinking, which is that falling in love with Mulvaney might be easier if you haven't actually met him.

CHAPTER 2

First Mulvaney Sighting

*N*ewsday's Suffolk County bureau took up the first floor of a stolid office building, design inspired by Joseph Stalin. I rushed inside, followed a sign to the newsroom, and found myself walking down a stark hallway, adjusting my black wraparound skirt, which had threatened to come undone several times during the long drive. I'd worried about dressing more formally and shouldn't have. Newsrooms are not known for their fashion sense or décor, but this one was in a league of its own. Bare pipes and masses of wires screamed "building code violation." The floor was a black-and-white checkerboard, last waxed before I was born.

Amazingly, everyone wrote on computers, clunky and rudi-mentary, but at least they had them.

At the *Knickerbocker News* we were in a "transition period," which did not mean we were trying to put our paragraphs in logical order. No, the *Knick*'s idea of transition was purely me-chanical and far from successful. After we typed our stories, an editor added odd symbols, which were then scanned by a computer that made more mistakes than the grizzled and oc-casionally amiable composing-room drunks it had replaced.

Not that *Newsday* had achieved technological perfection, either.

Touch-tone, for example, was not a concept embraced by the Suffolk County bureau of America's Finest Suburban Newspaper in the early eighties. All the phones had dials and all the reporters wore headsets that made them look like Lily Tomlin on *Laugh-In,* particularly the men.

It was a good thing I hadn't come to Long Island looking for a husband, Jewish or otherwise. All I wanted was to be in a place where I could cover good stories and where there might be some men who were presentable and not nuts. I had nothing against romance. But I didn't see why that had to dis-tract me from my work. Couldn't you have a torrid dalliance with a man who was not crazy and did not sap all your energy? I looked around at the men attached to those headsets and ruled out torrid. True, these men swiveled industriously in their chairs and dialed their phones ferociously. But they had pasty faces and sported bellies that popped the buttons of short-sleeved wrinkled white shirts in dire need of Clorox. These were not men you bring home to Mother, particularly my mother, whose taste in everything except her *own* hus-band, my father, ran to the flamboyant.

Newsroom? Gloomroom was more like it.

"Welcome to Long Island," said a gangly man who dressed differently from the others. But not necessarily better. He fidgeted with the wide buckle on the cloth belt of his mustard-colored leisure suit, the type that had been fashionable, briefly, in the seventies. He was, I suspected, that bane of all reporters, an editor.

"And to America's finest suburban paper," he continued, swigging from a can of Coke. "You're late," he said. As if it was a good thing.

I looked at him.

"We pride ourselves on our traffic," he explained.

"What am I doing here?" I said.

"Excuse me?" he replied, pretending to cough.

"I mean, what might you want me to cover?"

"Maybe Huntington."

"Didn't Walt Whitman live there?"

"Walt Whitman," the editor said approvingly. "They named the best mall in Suffolk County after him."

He pointed to a desk and I sat. The men around me stopped swiveling and dialing, smoothed their sorry shirts, stood, nodded, and examined my chest with what I suspected they imagined were surreptitious peeks.

Albany started to look good.

I took a deep breath, crossed my arms in front of me. They squinted in confusion. "It's yoga," I said. They gazed at me as if I had suddenly switched languages. "Gets me revved up to report."

I knew that some men at *Newsday* had once teamed up to write a very entertaining, very dirty book called *Naked Came the Stranger,* publishing it as the apocryphal adventures of a fictional suburban wife gone awry. Nobody here, though, looked capable of even dreaming about such a project. Maybe all the guys who wrote that book were in Garden City.

The editor in the leisure suit summoned me to a big table in the front of the Gloomroom. The City Desk. Except there was no city here. He handed me notes for an assignment about Ronkonkoma residents who were vomiting their guts out after eating at Local Clams, the orange-topped HoJo's hopeful I had passed on the way in. I turned toward the door, wondering if I should quit before he actually offered me a job.

A rubber band flew into the air. The editor retrieved it, then picked up a Suffolk County Hagstrom's and tossed it at me. He had the demeanor of a boy who had never been made to sit in the corner, a place he obviously belonged.

Unless you have Typhoid Mary on the loose, food poisoning rarely makes a great, or even a conclusive, story. Was it the chef's fault? Or the dishwasher's? Have the waiters been spitting on the orders? Did somebody have the flu? Is the place in question a dive or a culinary jewel having a bad night? With Local Clams I could eliminate the culinary jewel possibility. But I did not discount the chance that this was a trick played on tryouts, a test to see if I could make a nothing story into something. Into anything.

My thoughts were interrupted by a series of loud, quick stomps, an obscenity shouted into the smoky air, a round of cheers. I gazed up at yet another version of the *Newsday* male, better-looking than the others but potentially certifiable, just like the men I'd known in Albany. Not tall or dark but good-looking, if a bit Napoleonic. He wore a plaid short-sleeved shirt that fluttered in the air behind him as he stomped, more purposefully now, in the direction of me and Mr. Leisure Suit. He pushed by me and slammed his tapered reporter's notebook onto the City Desk Without a City.

"Excuse me," I said to the plaid back.

The back ignored me. "I speak to cops," he told the editor, slamming his notebook once more for emphasis. "Do not ever ask me to interview a police department *public informa-tion officer* again. I do not speak to *anyone* in public relations. I speak to cops, robbers, murderers, any level of mobster. I do not speak to PR men!"

I tapped him on the shoulder. "Excuse me," I repeated.

"Huh?" He turned. There was a coffee stain a few inches below his shirt collar.

"You shoved me." He had curly brown hair, flaming blue eyes.

"Who are you?" he asked, and looked me up and down. Unlike the other male reporters, he did not attempt to hide what he was doing.

Without waiting for an answer, he stomped back out the door.

"He walks fast," I said.

The editor stood still. I bet that didn't happen often. "Jim Mulvaney," he replied, "is, unfortunately, a great reporter."

I'll be damned if I am going to spend all this time on a book about my husband.

I myself went to Midwood High School, which had its virtues, even if being in Manhattan was not among them. Erich Segal, who wrote the best-selling book *Love Story*—and the movie, too—had been a Midwoodite. So had Woody Allen, although nobody remembered him.

My high school friends and I played a game called "it could be worse."

"Worse than here?" someone would ask. "*Worse* than Brooklyn?"

"Yeah." I'd giggle back. "It could be Long Island."

I'd never been to Long Island. But I'd met Long Island kids at summer camp in the Catskills. At home, they lived their lives skittish about the city and stuck in developments—stuck in development, too—where they regularly prostrated themselves so that their parents would agree to give them lifts somewhere. Lifts anywhere. I made friends with one of them and felt proud, as if I had boarded a UFO and discovered an amicable alien.

That fall I convinced my new friend to flee Long Island and visit me. Her parents drove her in and, when they left, I took her on the first subway we could catch to the city, down into that glorious rumbling darkness that does not exist in the suburbs. As the train doors opened, she clutched my arm and dug her nails in. Afraid of the Seventh Avenue IRT. It was the end of a beautiful relationship.

My parents' two-story brick house stood just past the corner of Avenue I and East Forty-eighth Street. It was semi-detached, or semi-attached, depending on your philosophy of life and whether you were standing in the shared driveway or on the neighbors' stoop.

If you did stand in that driveway and looked on a diagonal across the street, you could see Congregation B'nai Israel of Midwood, my parents' shul.

A bus ride away, Brooklyn College stood closer to Midwood High School than the shul was to our home. My parents, demonstrating full-blown shtetl mentality, wanted me to graduate high school, cross the street, and go to college.

I protested. Such an important rite of passage should, I argued, involve more travel.

"Manhattan would be wonderful," my mother agreed. "And you can still live with us."

It was in reaction to this that I wrote my first piece on deadline: a college admissions essay.

In five hundred words or less I appealed to the higher sensibilities of the State University of New York in Albany, a comfortable 162 miles away.

"*Had I not been so busy with my numerous and varied extracurricular and charitable activities, I would have no doubt aced my SATs.*"

I vowed that when I graduated I would get a newspaper job in Manhattan, a reporter's dream, the city with the best stories in the world.

CHAPTER 3

Tryout with *Stories*

No one had ever told the young manager of Local Clams not to talk to reporters.

"So you fry fresh seafood?" I asked. We were only a few miles from the renowned clam beds of the Great South Bay.

"No way," he replied gravely. "Ours come frozen from Maine."

When he blurted out the names and addresses of two sick customers, I thought I had died and gone to Reporter's Heaven.

Hagstrom's in hand, I located a bivalve victim. Giddy at the prospect of being interviewed by *Newsday*—and from throwing up too much——she threw open the doors of her aluminum-sided palace and made coffee.

I did not have the heart to tell her I was only trying out.

"Local Clams is my favorite restaurant," she said, giving me the only quote I needed.

"Why, I've been going since I was a girl."

When it rains it pours. Who knew Long Island had history?

At the nearest emergency room, though, the physicians all refused to comment, citing "privacy," as if they wouldn't cough up the goods on every one of their patients if some highfalutin medical journal wanted to study the bacterial implications of improperly defrosted bivalves. In the hospital lobby, I consoled myself with the best friend a reporter ever had, the local phone book.

The headquarters of the Long Island Baymen Association——LIBA——stood, like its address said, at the end of a dock.

To get there I had to walk past the rank and file, a bevy of baymen. Neanderthal peering, I concluded, was endemic in Suffolk County. They were still staring as I knocked on the sinister-looking door.

"Is this a subversive organization?" I asked the man who opened it.

His eyes——green——twinkled as he looked out at the placid bay and introduced himself as "LIBA's *Chief* Information Officer."

I twinkled back. He was tanned, with a graying beard, wide smile, good teeth. If he was chief, could there be more? I myself had no problem with PR men, particularly one like this. If I followed my own rule and believed only half of what he said, I'd be okay.

We discussed the importance of buying local shellfish.

Clams, though, were not an aphrodisiac.

"Do you harvest oysters?" I asked the bayman/PR man.

He said he didn't, so I drove back to Ronkonkoma. It was too close to deadline for a romance, anyway.

As I reentered the Gloomroom, a swarm of newly arrived assistant editors flitted around Leisure Suit, begging to edit the day's best story, whatever that could possibly be.

The editor swatted his assistants like flies. They were all male. His, though, was the only suit.

"I'm a natural for clams," one of the acolytes insisted. "Who's got the clams?"

"Fischkin," Leisure Suit informed them, as if I was miles away instead of standing right in front of him. "She's got the clams."

"Who's Fischkin?" the assistant asked.

Still ignoring me, he motioned the boys into a circle around him.

"Tryout with tits," he mouthed.

Didn't this place have a women's discrimination suit? Even the *Times* had one of those. I skulked over to my desk, reminded myself that I had been granted a coveted tryout at America's Finest Suburban Newspaper, and wrote quickly. These computers might be new but I didn't trust them.

I hit a button and heard a printer rattle in the distance. Before I could get up, one of the Men Who Didn't Write *Naked Came the Stranger* rushed over, shook his head, and pointed to another key: "Send."

So this was how a modern newspaper worked.

"Fischkin, get over here," Leisure Suit bellowed minutes

later from the City Desk Without a City. He was playing with
his own keyboard. The "Y" fell off and he stuck it back on.
"You call this piece of shit a story?"

Investigating clams—and then rewriting a perfectly accept-
able story about them—seemed like a day's work to me. So
after I sent Leisure Suit the "improved" version and answered
a few dumb copy desk questions, I said I'd see him tomorrow.
He shook his head and threw a ball of paper at me.

"Open it!" he ordered jovially. The newspaper union, I
knew, did not make him pay tryouts overtime.

It was *rumored*—to a reporter looking for a job there is no
word more depressing—that an unnamed state political figure planned to make a fortune selling high-priced disaster
insurance to people who lived near the Shoreham Nuclear
Power Plant.

A guaranteed *IPdoubleS*. Impossible to Prove Shit Story.
And, without a name, what was I supposed to do? Call up
everyone in the phone book and see who confessed?

No. That wasn't what this excuse for an editor wanted.

I was barely back at my lowly tryout desk when he made his
way toward me, taking a circular route. What he wanted to do
was stand at my desk and listen as I called my sources, so he
could see who I knew and what phone numbers he could
steal. How long, I wondered, would it take to break out of
this office and flee these suburbs altogether? Get to Queens,
at the least.

He shot a rubber band in the air.

"Thought you'd never ask," he said, although I hadn't.
"Stanley Steingut!"

My mouth dropped open.

"Big-time, huh?"

"Big-time, yeah," I said, trying not to giggle.

Stanley Steingut, now on a voter-imposed "hiatus from politics," had been a powerful Brooklyn assemblyman for a quarter century—and the speaker of the state Assembly in Albany.

Which meant I knew him from two places.

Even better, I'd been interviewing him since I was three years old.

I dialed Steingut's office in Brooklyn.

His secretary told me her boss was at a cop funeral; a local precinct captain had died.

"I knew you couldn't do it," Leisure Suit said as he bent over and tapped the letters on my keyboard. I examined this oddly dressed, twitchy man.

"Watch this," I said.

I asked Steingut's secretary for the number of the funeral parlor that had the cop, then pointed to the phone. "These prehistoric contraptions have a speaker?" I asked Leisure Suit. The editor nodded emphatically as he pressed a button on the console.

"Sweetheart!" Steingut's voice, hoarse from cigars and recognizable, boomed out over the Gloomroom. "How's ya pop?"

Some of the Men Who Didn't Write *Naked Came the Stranger* stopped typing and swiveled to listen. I waved at them.

"Stanley, I hate to make you confirm this . . ." Leisure Suit shook his head, flung a rubber band into the air.

Steingut's heavy breathing resounded throughout the Gloomroom as we chatted.

"Of course I'm selling people that insurance," the former speaker of the state Assembly boomed into the phone. "It's a public service." I ducked as Leisure Suit flung another rubber band, this one aimed better than the others, and wandered away.

When I hung up, the Men Who Didn't Write *Naked Came the Stranger* applauded.

I called Steingut's clients. They told me that buying insurance would move a nuclear disaster to the other guy's backyard.

"You should get some yourself," one of them urged before I had time to explain that I didn't have a Long Island backyard and hoped I never would.

I finished the story and pressed "Send" as Leisure Suit made another uninvited appearance at my desk and instructed me to meet him in his "inner sanctum," a hole in the wall behind the Gloomroom. The only furniture was an oversized desk chair that must have once belonged to a fatter editor.

"How'd you do that?" he asked.

"My father's been the president of Steingut's shul forever."

"Sounds Communist." He twirled his too-big chair.

"Would make the Kremlin weep," I agreed.

He completed another full twirl on the chair. "Fischkin, I like your work," he said as he pulled a thread from the upholstery.

I looked at him skeptically.

"Ah, the clam story. That was just a test. You didn't yell back. We like that here."

What they liked was running a prisoner-of-war camp.

"I'll let you in on a little secret, Fischkin, a professional secret, a reporter's tip." His chest puffed with journalistic pride. "If an editor is yelling at you, it helps to think about something funny."

A technique I had already mastered in Albany.

I closed my eyes and tried to imagine Leisure Suit without his leisure suit.

• •

The hotel where *Newsday* sent me for the night was not in Ronkonkoma but in another place, called Bohemia, which couldn't have been farther from the truth. One exit east on the Long Island Expressway; one more exit beyond civilization. I was now sure that I would be stuck in the middle of Suffolk County for the rest of my life. I drove ninety miles an hour hoping to break the curse and got a speeding ticket instead.

I fell asleep too fast and dreamed not about an editor not at leisure, as I had feared I would, but about a man robbing a train. A bank, too. Jesse James with a hint of a brogue. A blue-eyed Clyde Barrow without Bonnie.

When the posse found him, he said, "I do not speak to anyone in public relations."

My best friend, Claire Farrell, bristles when I suggest that perhaps she's the one who should tell *her* life story.

"My life is true," she sniffs. "You made up your life."

"You're confusing me with Mulvaney," I tell her.

"Impossible. How could I confuse two people who are so unalike?" Claire, like my mother, takes full credit for my marriage. But all she really did was suggest, during my early days at *Newsday*, that I get Mulvaney in the sack.

"Remind me again why that was a good idea?" I ask.

"Compatibility is boring," she says. "The two of you have a better story, fabrication notwithstanding."

"And what story is that?"

"Screwball comedy, like in the movies. You and Mulvaney are the perfect screwball couple."

I don't think this is a compliment.

"You can't stand each other," Claire says. "And you can't stand being apart."

"Doesn't sound like a very good movie," I say.

"It's an entire genre."

I review what I know about this and settle on my ideal couple. "Nick and Nora," I say, kind of liking *that* idea.

Claire shakes her perfect blond bob furiously. "Nick and Nora got along. Also, they were cool and calm."

Claire's hair used to be long and black, like mine. In middle age, though, she's acquired a new persona along with her new look: deliciously inaccessible. Faced with *The Jim Mulvaney Story,* I wouldn't mind looking that way myself.

"He distracts me from whatever I am writing," I say.

"He distracts you because you want to be distracted by him. And he wants to distract you. Didn't you learn that years ago? If you just give in and write about him, he will leave you alone."

"Wanna bet?"

CHAPTER 4

How Could You Be So Stupid?

I arrived in the Gloomroom so early the next morning even Jim Mulvaney was at peace. The boy wonder sat quietly, drinking coffee he did not spill.

At my own desk, a few rows away, I opened the newspaper to my Steingut story on page five. Nice.

Newsday was a tabloid, in form if not content, which meant that headlines and photographs went on the cover and the best stories of the day ran "upfront," on pages three through seven. If your story ran there, it meant you'd "got good play." Everyone said it like that, as if it was a sexual act.

As a tryout, I couldn't have gotten better play.

I read my story, sitting sideways. Without moving my head, I shifted my eyes back, far as I could. He was still there. I turned again to the front page—"Steingut in Shoreham Scheme"— and sighed to signal that good play bored me. I got good play often.

He stood, walked over quickly. Slowly, he held out his hand.

"Hullo, I'm Jim Mulvaney." He smiled but not with his mouth.

He looked down at my legs and quickly up again. His blue eyes seared.

They also steamed, accused, and sent troops to fight an ill-advised war.

"Go away," I said.

"You always so good at making friends?" He examined me as if he were trying to imagine if I could be interested in him.

I examined him back, trying to figure out if this was an act.

He was dressed for a stakeout: cop shoes, another dreadful plaid shirt, coffee stain in place.

"We've already met," I said.

"I don't think so."

So he had shoved me and did not remember. This Mulvaney wasn't merely a deranged Irishman. He was a de-ranged, *self-absorbed* Irishman.

"Barbara Fischkin," I said, knowing I shouldn't.

"Where'd ya come from?" he asked.

"Albany." I'd meant to say Brooklyn.

"Funny, ya don't look like one of those upstate broads. What'd ya cover?"

"Mario Cuomo," I said coolly.

"Oh yeah? Cuomo. I used to be his paperboy. The old *Long Island Press*. He lived in Queens, ya know . . ."

We were interrupted by Leisure Suit, who waved his arms

apoplectically and ordered Jim Mulvaney to a mob slaying. "Just came over the scanner! Better get there before the *News!*"

The fearless cop reporter, stained plaid shirt blowing in a self-made breeze, stomped out the door.

Leisure Suit sauntered back to my desk, carrying a wet tuna fish sandwich that left a leaky trail behind him.

"Nice breakfast," I said. "Better than clams."

"Fischkin!" Leisure Suit said, shaking his Coke can in the air. "Mulvaney needs help!"

Why did I think I would hear those words again?

"He's with Homicide. You, do the neighborhood."

Little Italy came to mind. It would be a long drive. But I was free. Free, free, free at last from the suburbs. Free from Leisure Suit and the wet sandwiches and imported clams of suburbia. I could smell the espresso and cannoli already. And I was still on my tryout.

"I'll call you when I get to the city."

"City?" Leisure Suit asked, pushing another piece of sandwich into his mouth. "What city?"

"New Yawk," I said. "Gotham. The Big Apple. Crossroads of the World." Why would the mob murder anyone on Long Island? And why would the *Daily News* cover it?

Mayonnaise dripped on my desk.

"Uh, we don't cover New York."

"Why not?" I asked.

"What for?" the editor asked back. He was genuinely puzzled. "I try to go there as seldom as possible," he added.

Forty minutes later I found myself covering, if that is the word, a tree-lined street in Huntington, Long Island. Nobody was home at the dead man's house. Nobody was home at any house on the entire street. Maybe the whole neighborhood was a Mafia front.

Still, I couldn't go back empty-handed. When in doubt, commit a small crime. I opened the dead man's mailbox, took out his letters, and copied down all the return addresses, then put them back. It wouldn't do any good. But on a tryout you had to, at the least, look like you were trying.

As I drove off I wondered where Huntington's real darker side could be. It had to have one. A small sign said "Police," and I followed it to a cop shack, a dilapidated outpost with peeling red paint.

"Got anything about the mob?" I asked the freckled officer.

"Nope," he said, peering down my shirt.

For now, I guessed, this was as dark as it got.

Back in the Gloomroom, I gave Leisure Suit the list from the mailbox. If only the key to this guy's hit was in his Long Island Lighting Company bill.

The editor put his hand on his cheek and opened his mouth, as if he could turn any more cartoonish.

"How'd you get this?"

"I opened the mailbox, took out the letters, and copied the stuff down."

"You committed a federal crime?"

"Isn't that what I'm supposed to do?"

Actually, I'd thought it was a misdemeanor.

He nodded. "Fischkin, I like you."

I looked up and saw Mulvaney listening in.

"Nice shirt," I said. "New plaid?"

He gave me a midnight blue stare. "Did ya talk to any cops?"

"Nah, I saw one in the shack but he didn't know anything."

"You didn't ask him anything?"

"Such as . . . ?"

I didn't like the turn this conversation had taken. This man Mulvaney had a look of pathological competitiveness on his face that was worse than anything I had seen in Albany. Mulvaney moaned audibly, too audibly. He slapped his hand to his head.

"Did ya even get his name?"

"No," I said. This man wouldn't merely lead you to a dangerous ski trail. He'd do *that,* then leave you there to die.

"Why not?"

"Mulvaney, that cop was Andy of Mayberry. On a good day. Today he might've been Barney."

"What's that mean?"

I couldn't believe that a human being could wear multiple coffee-stained plaid shirts and ask such a question. "Barney Fife!" I said, hoping to illuminate him.

His face turned red. "No! No! No! Don't you get anything?" His eyes went beyond midnight. "Those cops, they all know something. He just figured you're a rookie and he was putting one over on you."

"Mulvaney," I said. "That's *your* name, right? I am not a rookie. I covered the guy who's going to be the governor." I waved my hand and it knocked Leisure Suit's empty Coke can on the floor.

"Governor schmovernor. You're a rookie. Nobody in Albany ever taught ya that ya don't talk to a cop without at least getting his name?"

"I didn't need his name."

"Let's try this again." He pointed his finger in my face. "I assume ya can read, right? All ya gotta do is read the little tag on his shirt right up there. Name. Got it?" His finger had progressed to a spot in the air a sliver above my left breast. The more excited he got, the closer his finger came.

I guessed what would happen a second before it did.

"Ow," I said as he poked my chest. He pulled back but it was too late.

At least now I could identify what was in front of me: an Irishman trying to flirt. We were in the preliminaries.

"Hey, Mulvaney, didja go to Catholic school?"

He stopped. "Yeah, why you ask?"

"The nuns teach you to feel up girls that way?"

Leisure Suit picked his Coke can off the floor and cracked a grin.

"Huh?" Mulvaney said, blushing.

"Poke and withdraw . . . Vatican II? Right?"

A few of the Men Who Didn't Write *Naked Came the Stranger* joined to watch the festivities. More of this and they might finally be able to write their own dirty book.

"I coulda gotten something outta that cop easy," Mulvaney said. His voice cracked.

"Yeah, that's you. The soul of experience."

"Yeah, at least I know the basics of reporting. At least I can find a church in Brooklyn."

"Huh?"

"Brooklyn, it's the Borough of Churches. You don't even know that?"

His type usually claimed it was "a Jew in the Bronx" you couldn't find.

"Mulvaney," I shouted, "you're an asshole."

"I may be an asshole. But that's not the question of the moment. The question of the moment is . . ."

This was a man who would leave you to die on the trail and then tell everyone what a great skier he was.

He raised his voice louder than mine. "The question of the moment is: *'How could you be so stupid?'*"

My face burned. Leisure Suit slapped his knee.

I stared at Mulvaney, unable to speak. He was not going to ruin my chance to be a *Newsday* reporter, even if it was the last thing I wanted to be.

I went back to my desk. I sat down. I picked up the phone, put it down. I picked it up again, called the precinct and described the cop. I got his name, called the shack. "I'm new here," I said.

"I remember you," the cop replied. We chatted.

At Mulvaney's desk, I slammed down a piece of paper. The Styrofoam cup that held his coffee vibrated. "This is the cop's name," I said.

"What?"

"This is his home phone number. His favorite color is blue. His mother's maiden name is, incredibly, Crook—and I will never speak to you again for as long as I live, unless, God forbid, I have to dump you notes to make up for your generally marginal reporting."

"Huh?"

"Fuck the notes, I'll quit first," I said.

The Short Paperboy
A TRUE-TRUE NEVER-PUBLISHED STORY

The Paperboy rode his bike through Jamaica Estates, a lush, distant neighborhood of brick mansions shaded by mature oaks. He flung his product with precision, as he did every afternoon, careful not to hit any of his customers, particularly Mario Cuomo, a famous lawyer who people said might be governor someday.

The Paperboy never stopped his work to talk to anyone. But the Taller Boy who appeared, suddenly, on his own bike begged to chat with the Paperboy.

He'd heard that the Paperboy was the best in Queens.

"Wish I could learn," the Taller Boy said.

The Paperboy puffed his chest. Only his father, the Real Mulvaney, puffed better. He invited the Taller Boy to follow him to each house on his route and he did.

The next afternoon, the Paperboy delivered his papers alone again, but was amazed by how much he missed the Taller Boy. He wished he had asked him his name.

Later he pedaled back through Jamaica Estates for his weekly collections and imagined the clanging of new change.

His customers, though, were surprised to see him, since all of them had paid for their newspapers earlier.

"Your tall friend," they explained. "He said you got sick."

How, the Paperboy wondered, could he have been so stupid?

· ·

Mulvaney's eyes glare a sharp blue. "Go ahead," he warns. He is crumpling sheets of paper with ferocity. "Just go ahead. Then everyone will know what a bitch you really are."

After reflecting on our romance and its history, I have considered writing something other than a book. An affidavit, perhaps. Or a dossier.

CHAPTER 5

Two Prophecies

Despite Mulvaney's attempted sabotage, Leisure Suit hired me within weeks—and assigned me, as threatened, to cover the town of Huntington.

Still, I could rent an apartment in Manhattan and be there in an hour.

I was about to do just that, when I received a strongly worded "welcoming letter" from my sartorially splendid editor, urging me to "live where you cover" and detailing the terms of the Gloomroom's "probationary period."

The small cottage I found, in a nondescript neighborhood on the western edge of Huntington, was as close as you could get to the city and still be in Suffolk County. Unfortunately, it was still only an hour away from my parents.

In their semi-detached/attached brick house in the Flatbush-Midwood-Flatlands section of Brooklyn, my parents rejoiced. Compared to Albany, Long Island meant I was coming home.

"We'll now have a once-in-a-lifetime opportunity to connect," my mother announced.

I thought that was supposed to happen at childbirth.

My mother reminded me that I'd be returning in time to witness what remained of her maiden term as the first woman on the Board of Trustees of Congregation B'nai Israel of Midwood. She'd been appointed by the president, who was, as always, my father.

"Nepotism," she'd told me, "can be a useful tool."

At *Newsday,* the Men Who Didn't Write *Naked Came the Stranger* said that Huntington had a reputation for sophistication. The basis for this, I discovered, was one street in a tiny incorporated section of town, the *Village* of Huntington, awash in overpriced boutiques and boasting an art cinema that survived on grants.

Although this street was called Main Street, the real Main Street of Huntington was Route 110, a mammoth north-south thoroughfare, home to shopping centers and mini-malls and finally, at its pinnacle, the Walt Whitman Mall. A small sign indicated a back alley where the poet's house stood.

For the rest of the summer I searched for anything that could remotely be called a story in the environs of Route 110. When I was lucky, I found one on Main Street. Stories were hard to come by in Huntington. In Albany, of all places, I'd had more stories than I could write, a hoard of features that could run anytime within a span of months, if not years. I'd report them out and then, instead of offering them to the desk, I'd hold on to them for slow news days.

In Huntington every day was a slow news day.

Not talking to Mulvaney, though, proved to be easier than I had imagined, since he was never around.

I heard he was off in the city we weren't supposed to cover, on a mob murder that interested no one except mob cops, mob reporters, and, of course, the mob. Then he was at NYU, taking a weeklong forensics course with a group of Long Island medical examiners. How Mulvaney got into med school, even for a week—even to work exclusively on dead bodies—I couldn't figure.

The Non-*Naked* Men said that he had walked away from his college diploma; that he only needed to complete an independent study project on Thomas Pynchon to graduate from some boozed-up party school in Maine.

"And you don't think he made that up?" I asked them, my first sighting of a "Mulvaney-true" factoid. I doubted that Mulvaney had ever set eyes on a copy of *Gravity's Rainbow,* unless it replaced a cinder block in a plywood bookcase filled with Fletch novels.

The Non-*Naked* Men also told me, with a collective, voyeuristic gleam, that Mulvaney had taken his girlfriend to a mob party, where her primary function was to snap pictures of him and some mobsters that also captured a certain United States senator in the background. So Mulvaney wanted a girl who would make his stories better and take no credit. He even put her dress—reportedly short, tight, and black—on his expense account.

• •

When he didn't return from medical school, a notice went up on the bulletin board. He was now permanently assigned to Manhattan.

"I thought we didn't cover Manhattan," I said, thinking I was alone.

"We don't!"

I turned and saw a woman who looked like she might have once slept with a lot of important men.

"Only Female Assistant Editor in Ronkonkoma," she said, introducing herself. "I hope you'll join our sex discrimination suit."

Where had she been when I needed her?

"As for Mulvaney," she continued, "he's a police reporter and that's all he'll ever be. Fall in love with him and you'll be entertaining the Suffolk County Homicide Squad until you're a hundred and two."

"You must know a lot about entertaining," I said.

I felt an arm quickly pull me aside. "She's going to massacre your next story." Claire Farrell shook her head, and the worn terry-cloth band around her long black ponytail fell off and landed on the dirty checkerboard floor of the Gloomroom. She was beautiful and didn't know or didn't care, always a good attribute. She covered Islip, which was even worse than Huntington. Every time I talked to her, I wished we were in a bar and could order another round.

"It was worth it," I said. "I just hope she doesn't think I was defending Mulvaney."

"What's wrong with Mulvaney?"

"Nothing except he's a rude jerk."

"Only to people he likes," she replied.

"He must have made an exception with me."

"Guess again."

It worried me that I found this brief remark interesting. "He seems kind of thick. Bullish. He's a caveman."

"But he can also figure out the core, the heart and soul of people, even as they're expecting him to be throwing up Budweisers," Claire noted. "I'd go out with him myself, but he reminds me too much of my brother."

"I can't imagine why any woman would go out with him."

"You will," she said. "And you should."

I turned back to the bulletin board for other news.

Newsday was "upgrading"—what kind of jargon was that for a newspaper?—our desk computers so that the paper's "internal network" could transmit electronic messages. We'd be able to talk to the reporters and editors in Garden City without making a phone call.

Message Pending is what they called it.

Why didn't they just get touch-tone?

"Think of the extraordinary ways the reporters here will find to abuse this," Claire said.

"I don't know," I said. "Aren't these the people who didn't write *Naked Came the Stranger*?"

Mulvaney claims he can't remember his childhood. Other people, however, including certain teachers and school administrators, say they remember Mulvaney's early years all too well. In his adolescence, his parents, still married to one another, moved from Queens, hopeful that the reputedly elevated atmosphere of the village of Garden City might transform what could best be described as an "unusual" child, who was, to say the least, "not a traditional learner." But like the *Newsday* Suffolk bureau, Mulvaney was more Ronkonkoma than Garden City. His high school principal still refers to the fall Mulvaney entered ninth grade as "Black September," which seems unusually harsh for an educator. By the time Mulvaney was a junior, the principal had implemented an experimental accelerated program to get students—one in particular— out of high school in three years.

"At least I was interesting in high school," Mulvaney says. "You were probably well behaved."

"Mulvaney," I say, "if you think anyone well behaved would come within fifty feet of you, let alone marry you, then you are even more delusional than I thought and it is getting worse with age."

CHAPTER 6

Foreplay

I t was a late autumn afternoon, fresh and hopeful, a Saturday. I'd finished my part of the weekend shift and sent my story. As I waited for questions, I calculated, by computer, how many seconds it would take me to get to Manhattan.

"Transferring phone call to Fischkin!" yelled the clerk at the City Desk Without a City.

"Meet me at B'nai Israel one hour past sundown!" the voice on the other end ordered. This was not a source but my mother, who had to be kidding. A non-holiday Saturday night and she wanted me in shul!

"It will be fun," she insisted. "They're going to arrest your father."

I put the phone down. My father was a mild-mannered re-tired accountant who smoked cheap cigars and cracked dumb jokes. As far as I knew, he had no other vices, except my mother, of course.

Oh. He also did the books for Stanley Steingut's political club.

I picked up the phone. "This isn't a financial matter," my mother assured me, lightheartedness intact. She was a silver blonde with long fingernails usually painted red or pink. Or orange. "It's just Las Vegas Nite."

"It's illegal?" I screamed into the phone.

A gaggle of assistant editors jumped up in unison from the City Desk Without a City. I waved them away.

"Only a little," my mother said.

"I thought you had a permit?"

"We didn't need a permit. We had the precinct captain."

"The captain who died?" My mother assured me that Steingut had left that funeral arm in arm with the dead man's successor, who just had to "go through the motions" before offering the shul any favors.

Fuming, I packed my work knapsack. Had I not been so busy covering the action-bereft Huntington Town Board and sundry school boards too numerous to mention, I would have realized that Ida Fischkin as a B'nai Israel trustee was a disas-ter waiting to happen.

"Las Vegas Saturday Nite" was her baby, her maiden proj-ect. She'd sent out dozens of multicolored brochures touting this new weekly event as "the oldest established permanent floating crap game in New York." Like most false advertising, it worked, and within months B'nai Israel had the most lucra-tive assemblage of roulette wheels, poker, blackjack, and, yes, crap shoots of any Jewish institution in Flatbush-Midwood-Flatlands.

"They needed to arrest *someone,*" my mother had explained. "So I suggested your father, since he is retired and could use a hobby."

She was the only woman in the world who could envision an arts-and-crafts program at the precinct lockup.

"So come," she'd repeated. "We'll have fun."

"I have other plans," I'd told her, feeling only slightly guilty. Already I'd had enough of my parents. I'd also had enough of this strip-mall excuse for a newspaper. It would be good to get into Manhattan and look for trouble or, at the least, for some better male specimens than western Suffolk County had to offer.

As I wound my way through the last of the Soviet-style hallways of *Newsday* Ronkonkoma, my stride was broken by a swirl of coffee-stained plaid. I stopped dead in my tracks.

The last thing I needed.

Comrade Mulvaney back from Moscow.

"Shit," I said.

"You kiss your mother with that mouth?"

I had not seen him since my tryout, but I had rehearsed cleverly combative retorts to the pronouncements I'd imagined him making. No way was he going to leave me speechless again, not even momentarily.

"Actually, I was just thinking about her," I said.

"Something wrong with your mother?"

"Nothing's wrong with my mother. She's just having my father arrested."

As soon as I said it, I was sorry.

"Gosh." His blue eyes turned soft like a girl's and, for a

brief second, until I caught myself, I thought they were extraordinary.

How could he imagine I would fall for this, the quintessential reporter's trick? Feigned sympathy. Do it right and people will spill their guts, tell you things they wouldn't tell their best friends.

"He's not really being arrested," I said, lying. "It's all over Las Vegas Nite at my parents' temple."

If I was trying to link my family to the Rothschilds, I had just failed miserably. Mulvaney's eyes widened. He thought I had a father who gambled too much, and this seemed to intrigue him enormously.

"It's not that big a deal," I continued, wondering why I didn't stop. "My mother started this gambling fund-raiser at her temple and everybody came and lost a fortune, figuring the money would go to a good cause anyway. Then the cops started looking at it. If you ask me, *Kol Nidre* Night is worse."

"Isn't that when they shake down people on the holiest night of the year?"

How did he know this?

"The Irish are the lost tribe of Israel," he explained, his blue eyes full of himself.

I found myself running on about the precinct captain who had protected B'nai Israel from law enforcement snoops.

"But he's dead," I said.

"That's right," Mulvaney replied. "Wasn't Steingut at the funeral?"

The funeral that took place on the week of my tryout. The week, I reminded myself, when Mulvaney wondered aloud, very loud, if I could possibly be the stupidest human being on earth.

He examined me up and down. "Ya gonna go watch?"

"Nope," I said, looking away. "I've got better things to do."

"My father's a criminal lawyer. . . ."

His father, I'd heard, also knew Leisure Suit. "Steingut will get him out," I said.

"You believe that?" He shook his head. "This is the guy who tried to make money by creating a panic over Shoreham."

He never heard of Three Mile Island?

"Besides, Steingut owes my father."

Mulvaney tilted his head, and I realized I'd said too much.

In the Ronkonkoma lot, I got into my Nova, which sputtered, then started. For the first time that day, I examined the dirty blue jeans I had on. If I wanted to get into any of those clubs in the city, I'd have to go home and change. It would take me forty minutes to get there from Ronkonkoma and another hour before I finally hit Manhattan.

Off the L.I.E., I skulked up Route 110, down various side streets too boring to mention, raced into my oversized walk-in closet—an important Long Island architectural detail—and put on a short black dress, one I had paid for myself.

Back on the darkening and eternally clogged Long Island roads, I kicked myself for not taking the train, spotted the entrance to the Interborough Parkway and merged onto it, reasoning that I would get to Manhattan quicker if I went through Brooklyn. That in all my adult life I had never been able to drive through Brooklyn without stopping at my parents' house on Avenue I did not occur to me until I had backed into their narrow driveway.

From there I surveyed the tree-lined block of brick houses and, across the street, the shul, basking in the glow of more streetlamps than it needed. An old man drove up, dropped off his wife, parked his cream-colored Cadillac, got out. He stepped onto the wide patio and slowly pulled one of the building's heavy wooden doors open. He seemed to have some bounce left to him. Or was it merely the anticipation of Las Vegas Saturday Nite? I tried to imagine winding up with a man like that.

The next car, a beat-up BMW with what in the darkness looked like duct tape holding down the hood, skidded to a stop. A man in a plaid shirt got out, waved to me.

This was a bad dream. Clyde Barrow did not attend B'nai Israel.

Not without Bonnie, anyway.

It's an old joke, but people say they are surprised to hear that Mulvaney has a mother.

He does, though. He even speaks to her. More, perhaps, than she might wish, sparing no detail of his life and its complications, too many of them of his own making.

After he announces to her that I will be writing *The Jim Mulvaney Story*—although all I am doing is making notes in case I change my mind—she calls me. She wants to be mentioned minimally, if at all.

"You should put your own mother in the book," she says. "It's not polite to write a book about someone else's mother."

Mulvaney's mother did not let him watch any television programs that were not on Channel 13, otherwise known, in the days before PBS, as Educational Television.

"There," I say. "Finished with your childhood."

"You kidding?" Mulvaney replies.

Well, if he wants more . . .

CHAPTER 7

Las Vegas, Brooklyn

*M*ulvaney!" I said in a whisper that had the intensity of a scream. *"What are you doing here?"* The temple door was warped but it had slid open quickly, as if oiled for an onslaught of gamblers.

"Why ya whispering?" he asked.

"Because, Mulvaney, you just walked into my parents' shul!"

"I bet your grandparents went here, too."

"They didn't just go here. They built it!" Volume returned to my voice. "They survived a pogrom, escaped Eastern Europe, immigrated to America with three small children, and built this shul so that they would always have a place where sneaky Christian men couldn't find them."

"Shush, darlin'."

I felt sweaty, so I took off my coat.

"Nice dress," Mulvaney said, looking me up and down the way he had the first day we met, the encounter he didn't remember.

"Yeah and it's not on anybody's expense account."

A few of my parents' friends turned around and waved happily.

He leaned against the red velvet wall and looked across the small, chandeliered room. His blue eyes dewed with fake religious fervor. A garish green New York Police Department press pass hung on a chain around his neck. In Suffolk County all we got were small, cheesy white ones.

I wanted to kill him. "Would you please get out of here?"

"What, and miss a great story?"

"It's not a great story. My father getting arrested at his shul is not a great story."

I climbed the steps to the sanctuary. "Don't you dare follow me in." I turned and caught his eyes, fixed on my rear.

"Mulvaney! We're in a religious institution!" At the top, through the open door, he peered over my shoulder.

"How can you tell?"

A screen, red velvet like the walls, hid the wooden ark and its Torahs. Rows of bridge tables displaying roulette wheels and the remnants of poker, blackjack, and crap games—each now guarded by an NYPD cop—stood where the prayer benches usually did. Cops, in fact, flooded the place, looking as if they had raided the entertainment segment of a bar mitzvah.

The floors, walls, and tables glittered with blue and white confetti. Some specks had made it as high as the chandeliers, crystal like the ones in the lobby, except larger, as if this were the Versailles of Brooklyn, not a bastion of one of the most decidedly working-class Jewish neighborhoods in the borough.

The chandeliers had all been donated by the Fortunoffs, former members who got rich and moved their furniture store to——where else?——Long Island. Illuminated beneath the nearest, a group of polyester-trousered women, my mother's mahjongg partners, chatted ambitiously. One of them batted her false eyelashes at Mulvaney. The rest gossiped about their husbands, all of whom were in golf shirts, although none actually played. Their voices were animated, delighted. As shuls go, Congregation B'nai Israel of Midwood was Orthodox but not too Orthodox.

A founding member of the Board of Trustees held up a megaphone decorated with a Star of David.

"Folks!" he announced in an ancient voice. "Coffee and Danish are on the house!"

If the cops didn't close them down forever, Las Vegas Saturday Nite would be even more popular when word got around that it had been raided.

"Just not with my own wife!"

Through the din I heard my father asking for conjugal visits at the lockup.

A circle of cops loosened to reveal a balding, ebullient man in black horn-rimmed glasses and a navy sport jacket over a pink polyester golf shirt, a garment only my mother could have selected.

Unfamiliar, no doubt, with Henny Youngman, they all guffawed.

"Funny guy," Mulvaney said.

"So, Mulvaney," I asked, unable to stand it any longer, "how'd you wind up with the religion beat?"

"This is a cop story."

"You sure?"

"Yeah, a little cop told me."

"A little cop? Short, you mean, like you?"

"I'm five foot ten and a half."

"Yeah, but you think you're short," I said. "What cop told you?"

"Dunno."

"Forget to read his name tag?"

He flashed me a smile. But it was more eyes than teeth.

I watched as my father held up his bound hands in mock supplication.

"Jeez," I said. "Did they have to cuff him, too?"

Mulvaney put his arm around my shoulder. I squirmed out of it.

"Big-time gambler, darlin'. Wouldn't want him to get away."

"My father isn't a big-time anything. You know very well what this is. Las Vegas Nite at the shul. And that's all it is."

"No. It's more than that. It's also a great story."

"Mulvaney!" I said. "You write about this and I will arrange for whatever balls you have to be surgically removed if I have to do it myself."

I looked up and saw the rabbi.

"You kiss your mother with that mouth?" Mulvaney asked.

"You are repeating yourself. Worse, you're a creep. I told you something in confidence and you came here to milk it for a story."

"How do you know that's why I came?"

"Because you're telling me that's why you came."

"How do you know it's the only reason?"

I paused. Took a breath. Recovered.

"Mulvaney, don't try to pull that crap on me. Don't you dare flash those blue eyes at me and try to convince me that you came here to see me. I told you that I wasn't coming tonight. You came here because you wanted to write a cheap, easy story making fun of two old people and their shul. How low can you get?"

He shrugged, reached over, and brushed confetti from my shoulder. "This crap is as annoying as parsley."

"I mean it, Mulvaney. Write about this and I will never speak to you again, even if I have the world's greatest mob story that can only be written with your help."

"Do you?"

"No."

"Good."

I tried not to look at him. "If you write about this . . ."

"It's a great bright."

"My father is not a bright," I said. "He is not some short little feature story about the foibles of human nature, the cute corruption of local politicians, or creative uses of leisure time. He's just doing the shul a favor, taking the rap so nobody else has to. He's not even a Long Islander." I paused for effect and had my own turn looking Mulvaney up and down, as if I was assessing his journalistic qualifications. "The desk won't take the story."

"They will from me."

"This is a slap on the wrist," I repeated. "It won't amount to much." But as I spoke I knew this story was all that Mulvaney said. In the world of newspaper brights, my father was the Montauk Lighthouse. As a nuclear moment, he'd put all of Shoreham's disaster potential to shame.

"This could blow up bad, too. It could be bad for your father," Mulvaney said. "I'm thinking I should hang around."

I looked at my father. He gazed longingly at the cigars in his golf shirt pocket. A cop picked one out, unwrapped it, lit it, and put it in my father's mouth. I could smell the Phillies Panatela from where I stood. A barbeque gone awry, a dump burning to the ground. The cops, though, didn't seem to mind. I just hoped the ones at the precinct would be that nice.

One of my mother's mah-jongg partners walked over and asked if I was engaged to anyone yet. Mulvaney snickered.

The rabbi was next. "Evenin', Father," Mulvaney said, and I gasped. The rabbi grabbed his confetti-dotted beard and stormed away.

"*Mulvaney!*" I was whispering my screams again. "*He's not a priest!*"

At dawn one morning, the Short Paperboy discovered *The Modern Farmer* and it became his favorite television program, one he never missed. He'd wake up by himself, don a straw hat—a Mr. Green Jeans hat, but he didn't know it—tiptoe downstairs, turn the set on, and *LET THE SHOW BEGIN!*

"How could anyone not like *Modern Farmer*?"

Jim Mulvaney, defender of early morning agricultural programming.

"Mulvaney," I say, "it's not the show. It's your lack of normalcy."

He is actually taken aback by this comment.

"A normal kid who didn't get to watch enough television would sneak off to a friend's house for a dose of Howdy Doody. A really creative normal kid would go to an appliance store, someplace where they had rows of televisions for sale, all tuned to different channels! But you! You got up early in the morning to watch something *nobody* wanted to see."

"Best sex show on television."

Did I tell you that he went to Catholic elementary school?

CHAPTER 8

Dueling Ancestors

*B*arbara, *my darling daughter, who is your nice little friend?"*

It was my mother in full polyester regalia: striped pants with a flowered tunic.

For my father's arrest, she'd had her hair done.

She gave it a pat and it didn't move. Diligently teased and sprayed by a hairdresser in red capri pants—a male, I think— at the beauty parlor on Schenectady Avenue. "His matador look," my mother called it.

"Nice outfit," I told her. She only got sarcasm about other people.

"Thank you, dear. The patterns *blend.*"

Mulvaney swaggered up, extended his hand, and looked at her with the kind of blue eyes she had never seen in shul. "Jim Mulvaney from *Newsday*."

"Ah, you work with my Barbara."

"That would require cooperation," I said.

"As a matter of fact," Mulvaney said, "she's one of our most talented rookies."

I gave him a look. He had, according to Claire, been hired only a week before my tryout.

"Dave," my mother called out, waving to my father, her red manicured nails flapping in the breeze, "we've got a *real* reporter here."

"And what am I?" I asked.

"Chopped liver?" Mulvaney offered.

My father, still in cuffs, happily held his arms up like a champ.

"Well, Jim," my mother said. She put her hand on his shoulder. "What is it *you* do at *Newsday*?"

"I cover the Mafia," he said.

"Oh, how exciting! That sounds so much more interesting than Huntington."

"I'm investigating gambling rings. But from the gamblers' point of view. Really, it's a victimless crime."

"I couldn't agree with you more," my mother said sweetly.

The love fest was interrupted by cops transporting their "perp."

We followed the rings of cigar smoke outside.

"Don't worry, toots," my father called out to me. "Stanley said he'd be down in an hour."

As her husband of forty-three years disappeared in a squad car, my mother invited Jim Mulvaney home.

• •

I stormed across the street, flung open my car. Mulvaney grabbed the door and crooked his head toward my parents' house. "You probably need to call in. Copy-desk jerks. Can you believe some of their questions?"

"Ever heard of this new, modern invention?" I said. "It's called a phone booth."

"It would be easier to call from the house," he offered, as nice as could be. Nice like a snake. He was offering to let me use the phone in *my* childhood home.

My mother, key triumphantly in hand, turned back to us. "Hurry up, Jim," she said. "Or you won't have time to interview me before Dave is released."

I looked at my car, at my mother, at Mulvaney. I thought about what she might tell him, gently shoved him aside, slammed the car door, and turned toward the house.

"I'll make you both something nice to eat," my mother said as she led us toward disaster.

The three of us climbed the brick stoop of the semi-detached/attached house. As soon as my mother put her key in the lock, Queen Asta scratched at the door.

"Oh, my little darling," my mother cooed.

God, how I hated that dog. A smelly wirehaired terrier. Now it was barking. This animal belonged in the wild, or some wild other than Flatbush-Midwood-Flatlands.

"Queen Asta," I said bitterly. My mother had purchased the creature as soon as I left for Albany, denying it was a replacement for me.

"Her name is just Asta, I'll thank you," my mother snorted as she jiggled the door open. As soon as she did, the mangy creature jumped frantically into Mulvaney's arms as if they were long-lost lovers.

"My husband mispronounces 'Asta,'" my mother told Mulvaney, one hand petting the pooch, the other again on Mulvaney's shoulder. "He calls her Esther. Barbara thinks she's very funny."

I looked at Mulvaney. If he got *Kol Nidre* Night . . .

"Nora Charles is my ideal woman," he told my mother. "However regal Queen Esther may have been."

Figures he knows Dashiell Hammett, I thought.

"And why is that, Jim?" my mother asked.

"Irreverence is sexy," he said. My mother giggled. We followed her past the small foyer into the living room. She turned back to Mulvaney.

"Barbara is worse than irreverent," she said. "Ask her to tell you about the time she killed her kindergarten teacher."

"Mother!" I shouted.

"Really?" Mulvaney asked.

"No, not really," I said, annoyed. "The woman died reading us a fairy tale. I had nothing to do with it."

The living room floor, softly lit with Mediterranean lamps in a fruit motif, was covered with a bright green carpet that had enough garish force to make the blind see. On a side table, I spotted a framed photograph, my first-grade portrait. There I was, in ponytail and barrettes, still a free and functioning member of society, despite the dead kindergarten teacher.

That was more than I could say for my father at the moment.

Quickly, I pushed the picture facedown on the table. Was it my photograph or the seashell frame I did not want Mulvaney to see? My mother excused herself to get some food, and

Queen Asta, hearing the magic words, jumped out of Mulvaney's arms and followed her into the kitchen. Mulvaney looked stricken.

"She loves whoever feeds her," I told him.

He righted the frame, accidentally banging it against a purple grape—studded lamp. A small starfish fell off.

"You'll get better-looking," he said to the picture.

"Speak for yourself," I replied.

We stood by the couch, which was covered in plastic. Under that was a new slipcover, green like the carpet but with knobby purple stripes. My mother raved about "the convenience" of slipcovers. Then she encased them "just to be sure." The only thing this particular slipcover needed protection from was itself.

Mulvaney sat hard on the plastic and it rippled like a distant gunshot. He pulled me down next to him, a little too close. I pulled back. "Heads up!" he said. "Armed couch!"

"Screw you," I said as I stood.

"Must be on your mind."

"What?"

"Sleeping with me."

"Mulvaney," I said, "I wouldn't sleep with you if you were the last man on earth."

"Barbara!"

I jumped. But my mother was still in the kitchen.

"Not all women feel that way," he said.

"Put on some more lights, Barbara . . ."

It *was* too dark. I walked to the switchplate and noticed that my mother had "embellished" it, as she would say, with the same blue and white confetti from Las Vegas Saturday Nite. White lumps of Elmer's Glue popped out as if they, too, were part of her design. Mulvaney followed me with his blue eyes.

When he saw the artwork, he rolled them skyward, quick and sharp, but stopped on a dime as my mother, her mutt trailing behind her, returned carrying a tray with matching fruit motif coffee mugs and what, to the uninitiated, might seem to be pale, inconsequential crescent-shaped cookies.

"Jim, you must have some of my *mandelbrot,*" she said.

"Mulvaney," I said, "I hope you've got better teeth than your Irish ancestors."

My mother shook her head and turned to the task at hand. "Sooo . . . Jim, your family comes from Ireland?"

Where else could Jim Mulvaney's relatives possibly come from?

"How interesting," she said.

Mulvaney's chest puffed. He was obviously fond of his ancestors. I wondered how they would have felt about him.

Mulvaney began with the big picture. With him that meant going back at least a thousand years. This was not a man who dropped a grudge easily. Pagan rites. Irish uprisings against British rule. Brutal retaliations. He pushed on to the seventeenth century and to villages decimated by Oliver Cromwell, then on further to the Irish famine, which, he announced, may have started in 1845 but didn't end for five years. At least.

"The Brits caused that, too," Mulvaney told my mother. His eyes welled into a blue battlefield. My mother was transfixed. "Even if they didn't cause it, they didn't exactly do anything to stop it." Revision, I could see, delighted him.

We still hadn't heard about any specific Mulvaney ancestors. He probably believed he was related to all the Irish. Or they to him.

"Tipperary horse trainers," he said finally. "My great-great-grandparents. "Until the Spencers, that is, the *Princess Di* Spencers."

One should, I thought, be able to tell a simple tale about family history without invoking characters from *People* magazine.

"The Spencers took all my family's grazing land, and their horses, and left them with a small plot and hard planting." As he spoke he broke off pieces of mandelbrot and made it look like he was eating it, but without actually taking a bite. I'd heard from the Non-*Naked* Men that he could fake drinking a glass of whiskey with as much expertise. That way he could get an interview subject drunk, yet remain sober himself. "My great-grandfather hated that life so much he got on a boat to New York. You know the first thing he saw?"

"The Statue of Liberty," I announced dully.

"A sign that said 'Irish need not apply.' "

"How terrible!" my mother said. "I thought that only happened to Jews and black people." Queen Asta jumped on her lap and barked sympathetically, like the most reprehensible of newspaper reporters.

"Why don't you tell your own story, Mother?"

She looked at me, startled. I usually didn't encourage this.

Mulvaney, though, did not take the hint.

"Well, that kind of prejudice happened to my Irish great-grandfather," he continued. "But his son, my grandfather, wound up being so rich he held the patent for nylon during World War II. Actually, I'm thinking of moving to Ireland. But to the North."

"I'd never go back to the place I came from." My mother was, I hoped, gearing up.

But, as if he'd been launched like an oblivious rocket, Mulvaney expounded on about the Easter Uprising of 1916, the ensuing revolution, and the deal—a bad deal, he said—that freed most but not all of Ireland from British rule. "The six counties of Ulster are still ruled by Britain," he said. "That's because they had a Protestant majority there. But not for long."

"The British were not very good to the Jews in Palestine," my mother commiserated.

"In Ireland they wouldn't let people speak Gaelic," Mulvaney said. "In the North, Catholics still can't get jobs. People are getting killed all the time over this, but nobody in New York covers it. The *New York Times* covers Belfast from London."

"Jim," my mother said, "would you like to hear about my family?"

Finally. Now she would hang him out to dry.

I had heard my mother's real-life mythic party piece weekly, if not daily, since I was a little girl. The sentimentality, chauvinism, and melancholia, not to mention the violence, had practically ruined my childhood.

Still, it would blow Mulvaney out the front door. He was the type who couldn't stand it when anyone else told a better story.

But my mother had one. In a million years, Mulvaney, even if he made it up, could never match the historical heft or the emotional appeal of the tale my mother was about to tell.

Not with a few stolen racehorses. Not even if one of them won the Kentucky Derby.

My mother's story had drunken Cossacks, naive Bolsheviks, chicanery, fire, and mayhem.

It had six hundred dead villagers, including babies impaled on spears and children burned to death.

Even better, she was the star.

Like a myth-in-the-making, my mother, a six-year-old child who had been presumed dead, emerged unscathed from one of the worst anti-Semitic pogroms in Ukrainian history.

When my astonished grandfather saw her, he grabbed her in his arms and said it was not only a miracle but a sign. Now he was certain. Nothing would stop them from getting to America.

Mulvaney, even with Princess Di, didn't have a prayer.

I went upstairs and called the paper to see if the copy desk had any dumb questions about my stories, even if they were from Huntington. I also left a message for Leisure Suit: *"Mulvaney about to file bogus feature from Brooklyn, which is in New York City, which we do not cover."*

Bad news. My husband found an agent who wants to make a movie—and then a book—out of the Jim Mulvaney story. Look at any story that did not need to be told and there's an agent behind it.

"For example?" Mulvaney demands.

"Monica Lewinsky."

"Ahem," he says as if he is wearing a cravat. (As if he might ever.) "Ken Starr is not an agent."

"Yeah, but if it weren't for an agent, we wouldn't have had Linda Tripp. And if we didn't have Linda Tripp, we wouldn't have Monica."

Mulvaney found *his* agent at a bar, which is where he finds most things he wants, needs, or loses.

He reminds me that he did not find *me* at a bar, and this, I have to admit, is true-true. "I found you at a murder," he says, which is imprecise.

But it does reflect the ongoing criminal nature of our relationship.

On the night Mulvaney found his agent, he had roared into the city, singing rebel tunes, ready to mow down every British soldier on the Long Island Rail Road. Hours later he stumbled home and into bed, perfumed by whiskey, maybe Powers Irish whiskey, and fueled by affection. He placed a warm hand up my nightgown and touched me in the places men find when they want their wives to fall in love with them all over again.

That done, he told me he wanted me to talk to the agent in the morning.

"The agent's in from L.A.," Mulvaney said, as if a movie agent could be from anywhere else.

"I should have known you'd find an agent if you went to Elaine's."

"And why is that?"

"Nobody ever goes to Elaine's and comes back with anything really useful, like a cheap plumber or an honest contractor." We now own a house on Long Island, another thing I never thought would happen. After the Tiananmen Square massacre Mulvaney counted bodies in the morgues, compared his numbers with those of the Chinese government, and decided that even he couldn't be around liars of such magnitude. So we came home. Home for him, that is.

CHAPTER 9

Such Interesting People

W e left Felshtin, our little village. The only home we knew. We rode carts, and walked when we had to, through Europe."

My mother had reached her refugee segue.

"Somehow we got to Scotland. And in Scotland, Jim, we got on that boat without my father. . . ." Mulvaney looked bad, but not as defeated as I had hoped. Wouldn't it be unfortunate if, along with everything else, he could tolerate my mother?

"She's winding up this section," I said, but they both ignored me.

"My father had to come later because he had lice in his

hair. My mother was all by herself, taking three small children to America. I was seven by then, the oldest. . . ."

"You are about to hear about the ultimate spoiled brat," I said.

"Shh," they both replied.

"We were in—what do they call it?"

"Steerage," I said. She never remembered that.

"Upstairs the sailors were selling chocolate bars for a penny. Can you imagine that, selling them to poor immigrants?"

"I can't imagine that, Ida."

"Give me a break," I said.

"Shhhh," they both said.

My mother then launched into a description of a Hershey bar that was markedly nicer than anything she had ever said about my father.

"I told my own poor refugee mother, a woman alone with her three children on a boat to a strange country, that if she didn't give me a penny to buy one, I would cry until I went blind," she said. My mother's pride in telling this part always amazed me.

"What happened?" Mulvaney asked.

"I cried."

"And you got the penny?"

My mother nodded.

"Jim," she asked, "are you absolutely sure you are not an Irish Jew? Maybe you should check with your parents?"

Fortunately, the phone rang. My mother, whether she liked it or not, had finished her latest version of her life story.

"Three's a lucky number, Dave," she said into the receiver.

My father, I figured, was already at the Madison Club, Steingut's hangout and the bastion of Brooklyn Democratic politics. That was quick. Even better, Mulvaney had been wrong.

My mother put her hand over the mouthpiece. "This is his *allotted* phone call," she said dramatically.

"What," I yelled, "he's still there?"

"But it's okay," my mother held her hand up to stop me. "He's in a cell with two lovely transvestites."

"Such interesting people," she told my father. "And it will be a great story to tell at the next Board of Trustees meeting."

Now I could hear him on the other end of the line, doing a Stanley Kowalski routine, which was unlike him. He rarely yelled. Even at my mother.

She held the phone out. I stood to take it but she handed it to Mulvaney.

"The transvestites are wearing red evening gowns," Mulvaney announced.

I could tell that the "bright" he was going to write over my dead body had suddenly become brighter.

"What are transvestites again?" my mother asked.

My mother said she would stay home because she couldn't stand to see my father incarcerated, even if it had been her idea. "Steingut will be here soon, I'm sure," she added.

I walked outside in the cool, dark evening air to my Nova. Mulvaney jumped in front of me.

"Let's take my car, it's faster," he said.

I scowled.

"No girl has ever refused to ride in it," Mulvaney said.

"Do they all have duct tape fetishes?" I got into my Nova, smoothed my good black dress, and turned on the ignition.

Silence.

Mulvaney tapped on the window. "You have jumper cables?"

I shook my head.

"Can you fix a flat tire?"

"I don't have a flat tire, Mulvaney," I said.

I got out and followed him across the street. "You'll have to get in from my side," he said. The tape holding down his hood secured the passenger door, too.

"Wait outside until I slide over," I said.

"Fat chance," he said, sitting and giving me a pretend shove. "Broads do not order me around in my own car."

The car's upholstery was also beyond triage. "Nice to be king of the castle," I said as I inched in carefully. The ancient BMW started immediately. Mulvaney switched on a tape and the Allman Brothers blared. Along with its other virtues, his car, I noticed, had fold-down seats.

As we sped down Avenue I, Mulvaney coughed up what my father had said. The transvestites, apparently, had confessed all to the President of the Shul.

"You know Snooky's?"

It was a gentrified bar in Park Slope. "I once had a boyfriend who was the bouncer," I said.

"Figures a place like that would have some Jewish guy as the bouncer."

"And by that you mean?"

"Jewish guys do not make good bouncers."

"Mulvaney," I said, "my grandfather bit a Cossack."

"Your mother left that out."

"She tells the story a different way every time." He nodded and smiled.

Jim Mulvaney, connoisseur of inconsistent narratives.

The transvestites had gotten into an argument with a Snooky's customer, left in a huff, and made their way in a drunken, destructive haze up Flatbush Avenue, defacing billboards with pink Magic Marker and hanging garter belts from street signs.

"Actually," I said, "it sounds like fun." Clearly, I needed to get out of Huntington.

"Mulvaney?"

"Yeah?"

"My father's done some small financial maneuvering of the books at Steingut's club."

"I figured it was something like that," he said.

"No, that's not why he's locked up. But it is why my mother believes Steingut will get him out."

"Uh-huh."

"If you write a story about him, could you leave that out?"

"This is a bright," Mulvaney said. "That would ruin the tone."

He looked me in the eye. We were on Flatbush Avenue ourselves now. The traffic was heavy, but more cheerful and hearty than the L.I.E. and punctuated by neon lights in pastels and primary colors pulsating from the tops of stores that stood close to us on real sidewalks, instead of in distant shopping centers. Mulvaney slammed on his brakes to avoid hitting the taxi in front of us.

"Are you really going to Ireland?" I asked.

"Yeah, I'm going to cover the Troubles."

"The ones they already have or the ones you are going to make?"

"What do you think?"

What I thought was that he was lucky to have figured out not one but two ways to escape Ronkonkoma. Manhattan—and Belfast.

"Well, what do you think?" he asked again.

"I think you should take me with you," I said.

Mulvaney looked shocked. Certainly I had shocked myself.

"That was a joke," I said.

"Yeah. Besides, what would a Jewish broad do in Northern Ireland?"

Order Irish men to behave?

My breakfast is interrupted by Mulvaney, who sticks the phone in my face. "He says Hollywood will be fighting over us." The agent has a fake Texas drawl. Why do I think he also has a store-bought tan?

"So you're writing a book to go with the movie?"

"Do we have to stay married to do this?" I ask.

"Make up whatever you don't have or didn't do."

"Can I *do* something I wouldn't do?" I ask. "Like have an affair?"

Mulvaney glowers.

"We might need a little tension," I say, as if things aren't tense enough.

"Yeah," the agent agrees. "But make the guy up."

"I'm a journalist," I say. "I'm better off not making up anything."

Mulvaney puffs his chest and says that the agent represented Ed Koch.

"Mulvaney," I say, "nobody ever made a movie from Ed Koch's book."

He rolls his blue eyes, which is what he does when he wants the universe in general to understand that he has the patience of a saint. "That's because he didn't find Ed Koch until *after* he was mayor."

How hard could it be to find the mayor of New York City while he's still in office?

CHAPTER 10
Criminal Confetti

Inside, the Sixteenth Precinct reeked of the same industrial-strength cleaning liquid I remembered from elementary school, reigniting the homicidal tendencies I'd felt in regard to that kindergarten teacher, who'd gotten what she deserved.

A desk sergeant who looked like I expected Mulvaney would at fifty scowled as he motioned us over. His nose was red-veined; his stomach hung prominently past his belt. I held up my Suffolk County press pass and he shrugged.

Mulvaney flashed his big-boy NYPD version and the sergeant nodded.

"I want to see my father."

"Not so fast," he said, grinning at Mulvaney as if I weren't there.

I walked closer and stood in front of his face. "Then I want to see the new precinct commander!"

"The captain's having dinner," the sergeant told Mulvaney. "Howse your mother like you having a Jewish girlfriend?"

"Mulvaney!" I said, before he had a chance to answer.

"Mulvaney? You the kid of that lawyer in Queens?"

"Yeah."

"Great guy. He got my buddy offa some bullshit, trumped-up brutality charge. Any kid of Mulvaney's gets whatever he wants here."

"This how you got your job at *Newsday*?" I asked.

Mulvaney turned red. "Actually it was my father's bartender," he said.

He had to be kidding.

"I feel fer ya," the cop said. "But we all do what we gotta do. C'mon, I'll take you in there."

We followed him down a hall that smelled from more cleaning fluid, then another that just smelled from dead rot. At the end we found ourselves face-to-face with thick black jailhouse bars. My father, head down, sat behind them on a metal bed with a bare mattress, next to a steel toilet bowl that didn't have a seat. In the other bed, sleeping arm in arm, two men in red evening gowns snored loudly. When my father saw us, he put his hand on the bowl and lifted himself up.

"Somebody beat him," I said to Mulvaney.

"Why do broads like you always think that cops beat people?"

"Maybe because they hire lawyers like your father."

My own father held on to his pants. His belt was missing. It worried me that the cops thought he might hang himself over Las Vegas Saturday Nite.

"I need a Phillies Panatella," my father said, as if he were asking for his last meal.

I nodded, but I'd forgotten to bring one.

"Anything else?"

He shook his head and looked like he might cry. "I miss your mother."

"Daddy! You've only been gone a couple of hours. Besides, she put you in here."

A tear fell from my father's eye. He took off his glasses and shook them.

"Mulvaney!" I said. "Do something!"

We found the new precinct captain drinking his dinner around the corner at Keeler's Bar and Grill, which had a green awning and, inside, a pockmarked antique wooden bar. The captain himself was even more distinctive: a three-hundred-pound-plus six-footer with a large head and a full mane of red hair. He had a pint of beer in front of him, a shot glass of whiskey alongside it. "Daddy ain't gettin' out tonight," he said as he swirled unsteadily toward us on his wooden stool. "Nobudies gettin' out."

"My father can't sleep in jail." I tried not to look too closely at this, the latest offering of the NYPD. At least he made eye contact, even if his vision was as blurred as his speech.

"Yeah, Steingut was supposed to make a call," Mulvaney told him.

"Ain't nobudie made no call," the captain announced, emptying his shot glass.

"He's just an old man," I said.

"Shush," said Mulvaney.

"There's ex-ten-u-a-ting circumstances," the cop said.

"Like for instance?" Mulvaney said.

He leaned forward. "Like fer instance a mob connection."

"It was Las Vegas night at the shul!"

"Ya never know where these wiseguys gonna show up." The captain's words slurred more with each sentence. "Yah never know how they let each other know who they are. Red dresses, pink shirt, fer instance."

"Red dresses, pink shirts?" I yelled at him, incredulous.

"We gotta look fer all possible connections." The bartender filled his glass with more Bushmills. "Then there's the con-feddd-eee."

"Confetti?" I couldn't have heard him right.

"Shush," Mulvaney said.

"Ya know. Confeddee." He downed the whole shot. "Everyone with mob connections comes into the precinct these days with at least a few specks of that stuff on them. Blue and white. It's soz they can identify one another. Your father came in with the stuff all over him. Tons of it in his jacket pockets. We took the jacket as evidence."

"Evidence of what?" I asked.

"Shush," said Mulvaney.

"Nah. Glad you askt. His two girlfriends had the stuff in their pockets. In cahoots."

"Captain," I asked, "did you come up with this theory all by yourself?"

"That I did, darlin'. Gonna get me a commendation with it, too."

I looked at Mulvaney. He rolled his eyes. I rolled mine back and then was sorry I had. So what if we were able to identify the same human beings as madmen? It didn't mean we could stand each other.

I tilted my head toward the door.

Mulvaney ignored me. "I think you're on to something there, Captain." I'd been wrong. Mulvaney made no sense either. "It's like what happened with parsley."

The captain was sufficiently troubled by this modification of his theory that he pushed his shot glass away.

"Parsley was the Gambinos." Mulvaney plunged ahead and I wondered if he was about to make it worse. "Carlo goes to collect a debt and the guy can't make it, so he pays off with a parsley farm. Now Carlo's stuck with more parsley than he ever dreamed existed. 'Whatam I gonna do with all this fuckin' parsley?' he says, ready to shoot the guy."

As Mulvaney transformed himself into a mobster from New Jersey, the captain grabbed his beer, pulled his stool closer.

"Then the guy's brudda, he works for Gambino, comes up with an idea. 'We make people *buy* parsley,' he says. 'We make it indispensable.' Next thing you know, every Italian restaurant in New York gets a visit from a Gambino parsley salesman. Boom. Boom. Just like that. That's why you see a sprig on every plate, from chicken parmigiana to clams in red sauce. A plate'd look naked without it."

"Soz?" The captain moved his stool back and took a slug of beer.

"Well, you don't go around suspecting every guy who's got a little bit of parsley stuck on his lips after a big meal. They're not mobsters, merely victims. Victims of a mob marketing scam. Why, that parsley stuff, it sticks to you . . ."

"Like confetti," I said sarcastically.

Mulvaney looked at me, impressed. "Exactly, darlin'," he said. "You ask me, somebody has paid off a mob debt with a paper-shredding company. Forcing it down everyone's throat. Shuls, restaurants. Soon we won't be able to walk anywhere in this city without running into those little bits of confetti. The guys you got in there? They're not mobsters, they're the victims! The first victims!"

The captain drank the last of his beer. "Whadja say yer name is, kid?"

Mulvaney told him.

"Yeah? You the kid o' that big-time cop lawyer? Whatta they call him?"

"The Real Mulvaney," Mulvaney said, not without sarcasm.

"Yeah, that's it. Nice guy. He spends mosta his time at my cousin's bar in Rockaway."

"I know," Mulvaney said. "I saw *your* name on your shirt."

The transvestites walked out of the lockup and kissed Mulvaney, who did not kiss back. My father followed, with a bounce again in his step, if not in his now heavily wrinkled pink shirt. He told Mulvaney he was a genius.

"And me?" I asked.

"Chopped liver," my father said. But he was laughing.

At home my mother kissed her husband as if he had been gone a month and went upstairs to draw his bath.

I was left alone in the living room with Mulvaney, in the midst of an uncomfortable silence and surrounded by horrifying décor.

"I need a drink," I said.

Mulvaney nodded. "Maybe we should assess the damage at Snooky's?"

"I don't know the bouncer anymore," I said. "And what makes you think he was Jewish?"

I tried my Nova, which started, so I drove away. He was, I noticed, right behind me down Avenue I, but I lost him on Flatbush, didn't see him when I turned on Seventh. Snooky's was still open but there was no sign of mayhem of any sort, and as I ordered a gin and tonic at the smooth oak bar, I wondered if Mulvaney might have fabricated the entire night.

When he appeared, I ordered him a Bushmills.

"Captain Tubridy's best friend," I said, handing it to him. "And thank you for freeing my father."

He moved his own stool closer.

"Mulvaney," I asked, "are we trying to have a romantic event?"

He did not answer.

"Or avoid one?"

Again, he did not answer. Perhaps, I thought, he really is Irish.

Unlike the Mulvaneys, the Fischkin family does not come with its own bartender.

We do, however, have a cousin who used to be Ed Koch's PR man.

Cousin George is the second PR man to be depicted in this book I may or may not be writing, which should tell you just how far the average journalist would get without the public relations industry.

"My husband wants me to write about him," I say to Cousin George, who now has his own firm, close, though, to Gracie Mansion. I do not ask him why there isn't an Ed Koch movie.

"Do not forget Tiananmen Square," he says. A good PR man, he reminds me, could do a lot with that anecdote.

"But all he did was cover it," I say.

It's true-true that Mulvaney was courageous in Tiananmen Square. Stubbornly so. He did not leave when the tanks were rolling and hide upstairs in the *Newsday* apartment, even if it did have a perfect view. He stayed in the square, even after a People's Liberation Army kid-soldier put a gun to his head and then shot a Chinese guy instead.

Still, as Mulvaney's potential biographer, I must point out that his was not the only life spared that day.

And when Beijing calmed, he could—and did—leave it for the pristine luxury apartment we rented in Hong Kong. True-true, he had very bad dreams every night. But then another story came along. Sure, Tiananmen Square still plays on in Mulvaney's brain. But he thinks about it in terms of his memoir. On a list of career achievements, his near miss at the wrong end of a gun transforms into a bullet, but not a real one:

- Covered Tiananmen Square.

American foreign correspondents are not supposed to become part of the story.

Once in a while, though, that quick gun to the head turns from a threat into an arrest or an abduction or worse and the journalism community comes out in full, supportive force. For a while.

Ultimately, though, reporters who become part of their stories do not win Pulitzer Prizes. Not even the ones who are killed.

CHAPTER 11
Premium Chocolate

I left Mulvaney at the bar that night and didn't see him in Ronkonkoma. Weeks passed with no Mulvaney in the Gloomroom. A few of his mob stories from Manhattan ran, but the one about my father's transvestites didn't. I asked Leisure Suit if Mulvaney had even written it, but the editor waved me away because an injured twelve-ton sperm whale had washed up at Robert Moses State Park.

"This is big!" Leisure Suit announced. "Very big!"

Dumb, too. It was almost winter and that whale was stuck on Long Island when it should have been in Mexico.

Mulvaney's whereabouts were as hard to figure. He had

forced me to notice him in any number of ways, including springing my father from a lockup. Then he'd disappeared. Maybe he liked to have women fall in love with *him* as long as he did not have to fall in love with *them*. But that was not a Mulvaney trait mentioned by the Non-*Naked* Men.

The only one who had any news about Mulvaney was my mother. She claimed he had stopped by the house while she and my father were at an emergency meeting of the B'nai Israel Board of Trustees. They needed to find a new name for Las Vegas Saturday Nite. "Something that will attract less law enforcement speculation," she explained. "I think we should call it 'Bingo' and have a winking-eye logo. The rabbi likes '*Jerusalem* Saturday Nite.' He says that since the state of Israel has to gamble for its survival, people will get it."

Attempting to sound casual, I asked her how she knew Mulvaney had been there.

"Well," she said, "he left the largest box of Godiva chocolates on our front steps. . . ."

Why was he still buttering up my mother?

"Unlike you, he actually listened to my story. That's what makes Jim Mulvaney a great reporter."

Newsday's accountants—who derived their power from terrifying editors—ordered Leisure Suit to give me four days off before the end of the year. As I contemplated a quick vacation getaway, I considered leaving Long Island, never to return. Be smarter than that whale, I said to myself.

The whale remained on the beach and now Leisure Suit wanted to give it a name.

"Something with stature," he said.

"How do you say 'humongous almost-dead whale' in Latin?" I asked him.

He stood, applauded, ordered the paper's librarians to do some quick research, and put in a rush order for "*Physty Lives*" T-shirts for the Gloomroom. "Physty," the editor said, was short for *Physeter macrocephalus,* which actually meant humongous *toothed* whale. He was delighted with himself. But when the shirts arrived, they sat in a box by the City Desk Without a City. No reporter would take one, let alone put one on, prompting Leisure Suit to summon Mulvaney back from the city. "Mulvaney will wear anything," he told us angrily.

"Mob's into blubber?" I called out when I saw him at the desk behind me, sweet as could be. Even Mulvaney couldn't spoil my mood. It was the end of the Saturday shift and in minutes I'd be out of the Gloomroom for four glorious days.

"You're welcome for the chocolates." He had slipped a Physty T-shirt over his latest plaid. His chinos were too long and hung over his cop shoes.

"The chocolates were for my mother," I said.

He tried to smooth the crumpled notes he was supposed to dump to me, then stood and walked to my desk. I pretended to concentrate on my computer.

"That's not why I gave them to her."

"We have to do this quickly," I said.

On my screen, I called up the *Long Island Budget,* which was a fancy title the editors gave to their daily list of story summaries, proving once again that newspapers might rail against jargon but they all had their own.

RONKONKOMA BUREAU

Physty Lives
Typically the Suffolk County Police Department and "Animal Rights Are Us/Long Island," a humane society off-shoot, have more trouble getting along than Catholics and Protestants in Northern Ireland. . . .

"Mulvaney, did Leisure Suit let you write your own budget note?"
"How'd ya guess?"

But now, fighting for a common good, to keep a sick whale alive, they have bridged their ideological differences and created a fragile, although workable, peace.

He hated this as much as I did.
"Mulvaney, if I tell you it's very funny, will you hurry with those notes? I have a plane to catch."
"Where?" Mulvaney asked, looking like he might want to go.
"Where that whale should be," I said. "Mexico. Isla Mujeres. Island of Women."
"Some Bella Abzug junket?"
Not, I guessed, a name he mentioned often.
"No, I'm merely hoping it's an island without men."
"You broads are all the same. But when it comes down to it, most of ya don't even know how to change a flat tire." He was back to that car-fixing theme again. Why didn't he just get a job as a grease monkey? "Nothing makes a women's lib-ber angrier than having to call a man to fix a flat tire."

Women's libber? I couldn't believe he'd actually said that. This was the 1980s. Maybe he *was* destined to spend his life with the Homicide Squad.

He looked down at his notes again. "You gonna bring me a present?"

"Whadya want? A Mexican girl slave?"

"Just my type. Raven black hair, high cheekbones." He stopped, looked at my face. I knew I was supposed to be flattered, but if I did that, I'd miss my plane.

"Nah, too much trouble," he said. "I'll take a bottle of mescal."

"With a worm?" I asked, typing as fast as I could.

"They all have worms," he replied, eyes flashing.

"Not on the Island of Women, they don't."

A half hour later, notes dumped, story written, my preparations to leave were interrupted by Leisure Suit leaping into the air.... "Our Physty's made a miraculous recovery!" he shrieked.

I darted out of the newsroom.

"I'll need another Sunday reporter!" Leisure Suit shrieked again. "To cover his *dramatic* return to the Atlantic Ocean!"

"Fischkin can do it!" I heard someone snicker in the distance. The unmistakably gleeful voice of Jim Mulvaney, boy reporter.

Claire followed me into the hallway. "Run as fast as you can, but don't forget to come back!" She put an oversized sombrero on my head. "Stolen from the 110 Taco Bell," she announced.

"What was Mulvaney doing?" I asked her. "Trying to ruin my vacation?"

"No, dummy, he was making a pass at you."

• •

In Mexico, on the beach, I read *The Executioner's Song*. Nothing relaxes like a cheery dose of Gary Gilmore via Norman Mailer. I was interrupted, though, by the appearance of José Luis Something-or-Other, a handsome, tall, *male* resident of the Island of Women. He claimed he'd just gotten out of military prison in Veracruz, where he did time for beating up his commanding officer.

I was amazed at how far my high school Spanish took me. I was not amazed when José Luis Something-or-Other, his story told, his semen spent on the beach one steamy night, had nothing left to recommend him. I returned to Gilmore-Mailer, but the overriding criminal aspect of it all—and the specter of José Luis's combative past—made me imagine I was seeing plaid shirts in the Yucatán sand.

Mulvaney wants me to take the Mexican out of this book I am not writing about him.

"But he was real," I say. "And a telling choice. I left you at *Newsday* and slept with a thug."

My husband views this book as an opportunity for me to let the world know how wonderful he is. I, on the other hand, think it should be a reflection, an exercise in introspection. Over the years, Mulvaney has kept me too busy for much introspection.

"You already know how it turns out," Mulvaney says.

"But I don't know if I was right. I need to know before I go into the twilight of my years, the Ida-Dave phase, if the distractions of this marriage are what has kept me down or made me whole."

"You were right," he insists.

"We'll have to see how the *book* turns out," I reply.

CHAPTER 12

Flat Tire

Tanned but haunted, I returned to Ronkonkoma, where it was snowing. On the drive in, news radio was all over the murder of John Lennon. But that had happened in Manhattan, which we didn't cover.

In Ronkonkoma, they were still on the whale. Leisure Suit's ebullience notwithstanding, it hadn't budged an inch off the shore of Robert Moses State Park.

Maybe that whale was just enjoying the publicity.

I'd tried to convince Leisure Suit to let me look for stories in Huntington, *then* come in. But he always wanted to see his reporters before they started their day. This was especially true when you came back from a non–Long Island vacation.

It was as if he knew what you were really thinking: Could I cover Huntington from Isla Mujeres?

Mulvaney looked as if he hadn't moved from his Ronkonkoma desk. He'd shed his Physty T-shirt, but the green and yellow plaid he wore was familiar.

"Isn't that whale dead yet?" I asked him as my own phone rang.

Leisure Suit, elevated by his role as a revered nature editor, was calling from the City Desk Without a City twenty feet away. How much worse, I wondered, will it be when he can do this electronically with the long-threatened but yet-to-appear Message Pending? He must have heard me thinking because he sent me right back to Huntington to cover the new cesspool regulations. It was, literally, a piece-of-crap story.

Later, back in Ronkonkoma, I wrote three hundred words and left too annoyed to speak to anyone. And by that, I meant *anyone*.

To get home I took the L.I.E. for the fourth time that day. Its temperament had not improved either, since morning.

I got off at Route 110.

It was just past the out-of-business Times Square Store that my Chevy Nova began sinking to the right.

A flat tire. The perfect end to a perfect day.

I saw what I thought was the entrance to Taco Bell but drove, instead, over a median covered with slush. With that, the last bit of useful air rushed from my tire.

Inside, fake Mexican teenagers served fake Mexican food and I wished for *camarones en ajo,* like the ones I had eaten only days earlier.

I didn't have a jack.

Fortunately I had a quasi-brilliant idea.

"Mulvaney!" I said into the pay phone.

"Yeah?"

"You know who this is?"

"Yeah." He stretched out that one-syllable word.

"So you're still hot on the whale trail?"

"Ya got a better story?"

"I do," I said.

A half hour later, he sped into the parking lot of the Huntington Station Taco Bell and slammed on the brakes. He got out and gave me a quick, very quick, kiss on the lips.

I had never been kissed that quickly before. This surprised me. Although it shouldn't have.

"Tastes like an unsavory Mexican," Mulvaney said.

"You're a terrible reporter," I replied. "I spent the week with Norman Mailer."

"What's the story?"

"The story," I said, nodding to my Nova. "First Feminist on Earth Not Enraged After Calling Man to Fix Flat Tire. Front page, right?"

He rolled his blue eyes. "Only one problem. In the midst of your history-making lack of vitriol, you forgot to tell me to buy a jack."

"*You* don't have a jack?"

"Wait a minute." He opened the trunk of his BMW. Amid a dozen used Styrofoam coffee cups, a pile of dirty plaid shirts, and a dog-eared copy of Jim Bouton's *Ball Four* sat a bulky black bag, the kind doctors used to carry when they still made house calls.

"You steal that bag from Marcus Welby, Mulvaney?"

"Who's Marcus Welby?"

"Forget it. Where'd you get the bag?"

"Medical examiner's school. The coroners all chipped in and bought it for me. In lieu of a degree. It's great in the rain."

"It's not raining," I said.

"Nope."

"And you don't have a jack?"

"Nope. And you don't either."

We drove to my cottage, transported by duct tape, nothing more.

"So how'd you kill your kindergarten teacher?" Mulvaney asked.

"I did not kill my kindergarten teacher," I said, and moved closer to the door. "Do you think I'll fall out if I lean against this heap?"

"Depends whether you're guilty of homicide or not."

"I told you, she was reading us a story and she had a stroke."

"What story?"

" 'Hansel and Gretel.' I think she keeled over when the witch lost."

"She identify with her or something?" He pulled me closer to him. "The door could fall off, you know," he said. "Duct tape is not the world's most secure adhesive."

I pulled away. "If she didn't identify with the witch, then she should have."

"So you did kill her." We were at a red light on a dark stretch of Route 25A. Mulvaney switched on his brights.

"Well, I might have wished her dead once or twice, but I didn't kill her." For reasons I did not understand, I prepared myself to tell him everything about P.S. 203 in Brooklyn and

the meanest kindergarten teacher in history. My mother—
and her distinctive fashion sense—was involved, of course.

Then we rounded a bend and—at what any driver's educa-
tion teacher would have declared an inopportune moment—
Mulvaney leaned over and kissed me, on the lips but slow this
time. And long.

I kissed back, bracing for the crash.

"Mulvaney," I said when we were done and still on the road,
"do all minor homicides have the same effect on your libido?"

"Nope," he said. "Only when I get a confession in the bar-
gain."

"I didn't confess to anything," I said as I leaned back on the
door.

On the cold rocky beach down the street from my cottage, an
entire bottle of Mexican mescal disappeared. Even in the dark
I could see Mulvaney's eyes as he shook the worm out of the
bottle, bit it in half, and put the other half in my mouth. We
tried to identify stars, then the winds started so we went inside and fell asleep. I woke first. It was still dark. "*Newsday*
makes us work too hard," I said as I pulled down the zipper
on his pants.

"I'm kind of attached to someone," he said. I ignored that
and kept doing what I was doing, since the idea of Mulvaney
attached to anyone except himself was unimaginable.

Still, I had never seen a man look so blatantly triumphant
when faced with a woman, undressed.

We bought a jack on the way to work, stopped at the Taco
Bell to put the spare on my car, and eventually walked into the

Gloomroom separately. We didn't need to tell one another that it would be a good idea to keep the romance a secret. We worked with people who, like us, spent their lives reporting other people's miseries, victories, mistakes, and emotions. That we had just slept together would be one more story, dissected unmercifully. We knew, too, that we were fooling ourselves if we thought no one would find out. Newspapers, even Long Island newspapers, were a lot like Brooklyn shuls when it came to secrets, which is probably why I felt so comfortable working as a reporter. Everyone at B'nai Israel knew my father had fixed Stanley Steingut's books. And within four hours of our arrival that morning, everyone at *Newsday* Ronkonkoma—except Leisure Suit, of course—had guessed that I had slept with Mulvaney.

After we filed our stories, he walked the four feet to my desk and waved Islanders tickets in my face. I assessed how long I'd be able to stand the sight of grown men crashing into one another, grabbed my knapsack, and threw in a book by Erica Jong. But not *Fear of Flying*.

The romance was no less complicated than the flirtation, even though we avoided my parents. On Long Island, during that winter and the months that followed, we lived a bicoastal existence: my North Shore cottage; his South Shore bungalow, with a few delightful forays to Pier 92 in Rockaway, Mulvaney's father's favorite hangout, owned by his best friend and bartender, Dan Tubridy.

Pier 92 was lodged between a broken-down bait shop and a McDonald's and had no sign, as if the Tubridys refused to acknowledge that Prohibition had ended. But inside there was an oak bar with a stunning view of Jamaica Bay. I liked Dan

Tubridy so much that I wondered if my parents' new police captain had lied about being a Tubridy cousin, despite the name on his shirt. Maybe he just hoped he could be one.

The Real Mulvaney, Mulvaney's father, wasn't a bad guy either, not once he explained that he didn't believe in defending brutal cops as much as he believed in defense, period. Was he more real than his son, though? That I couldn't imagine.

Mulvaney, my Mulvaney, lived in Long Beach, a faded resort on the Atlantic Ocean. In its heyday it was home to Rudy Vallee, Eddie Cantor, and the silent screen stars Vernon and Irene Castle. By the 1980s the longtime locals had to be satisfied with Mulvaney and a bevy of deinstitutionalized psychiatric patients, who filled what were the once grande-dame hotels on the boardwalk. One day Woody Allen invaded one of those broken-down mansions, sent the patients to their rooms, and made a movie. "Woody Allen went to my high school," I informed Mulvaney.

"Oh yeah? Did he ever visit?"

"Yep," I said, lying.

Mulvaney's bungalow was a disaster area, too. He kept house like a fugitive or a refugee. Everything he owned was thrown on the small living room floor, ready to be grabbed in case of a quick getaway. He had no affinity for closets or even drawers, and I knew that I would never live with him without hiring a maid. If I had to spend my life cleaning up after Mulvaney, I would never get any of my own work done.

Mulvaney is pouring red wine for me.

He knows I like the way he pours.

"Remember this song?" he asks as a Rosemary Clooney CD plays.

"I remember the whole jukebox," I say. I can, in fact, see back twenty years to the bar where he found it, a dive in Huntington, near the Long Island Sound. Mulvaney spotted the jukebox in a corner of the cloakroom. When he plugged it in, it worked.

In the depths of his being, Mulvaney is an investigative reporter and that is how, a decade ago, he won his Pulitzer Prize. It wasn't for investigating foreign countries. Although what he looked at was certainly foreign to him.

Jim Mulvaney won a Pulitzer Prize for closing down a Southern California fertility clinic.

He proved that its doctors had stolen eggs from the female patients they had failed to impregnate, then inserted them in the wombs of other, hopefully luckier, women.

And so one day Mrs. Smith spotted Mrs. Jones at the supermarket, looked at the new Jones baby—which she did not know had been conceived with her eggs—and said:

"If I could only have a child, it would look like that."

Mulvaney discovered all this with only one week of medical school under his belt. And without ever watching one episode of *Marcus Welby*.

Mulvaney is also an investigative romancer. I'd always hoped for a man who would sing to me. But that is not

Mulvaney. He charms by finding things. Or by reminding me what he once found.

"I'm not trying to force you to do this book about me," he says. "But if they make a movie and a book, then you'll have enough money to write about whatever you want."

How many writers have heard that before?

CHAPTER 13

Teamwork, Part One

Mulvaney, his head propped on my pillow, a cup of black coffee he'd made himself steaming on my night table, dialed the first Suffolk police precinct.

"Hullo, Sarge. How ya doin'? Whodayathinkitis? Any good murders last night? Nope. Okay. Thanks. Bye."

Hang up. Dial. Repeat with next precinct.

Resting was not something Mulvaney did, even in bed.

He talked as fast as he walked, and a juicy homicide made his day.

A prominent victim was good, a celebrity suspect better, although even an Everyday Joe with the right, distinctive, non-boring act of desperation could do the trick.

I got back into bed. "I'm sorry nobody killed anybody, Mulvaney."

"Better no homicide than a dull one. There's nothing worse than boring desperation." He put a hand up my thigh. "Time wasted when I could be checking out the mob."

Storywise, he'd had plenty of boring desperation lately. A loose alliance of Long Island car thieves—not a mob although they wished they were—had captured the attention of Leisure Suit. This was no coincidence. The editor had just bought a new Mazda. "I don't do car theft," Mulvaney had told him. But to no avail.

The Mazda was red and as souped up as its owner. "Do you think Leisure Suit has a girlfriend?" I asked Mulvaney.

The phone rang. He picked it up. Indignant, he handed me the receiver.

Well, it was *my* bed.

"Barbara! I hope you speak Spanish!"

I sighed. The PR man from Huntington Hospital was not, I knew, calling with an untimely fatality, an uncured illness, or even a bad accident. Happiness was all you got from this guy, even if he did work for a medical facility.

"Spanish? It's one of my languages!" I told him as he described a potential non-story with agonizing precision.

In the cavern that was my walk-in closet, I slipped on a pair of jeans, wondering if I couldn't do this one by phone. Mulvaney watched as I zipped up. "Since when do you speak Spanish?" he asked.

"*Un poquito en escuela*," I said, confessing to him yet again.

• •

According to the PR man, there'd been a nonfatal fire in a "commercial/residential building"—an apartment over a store—followed by a commendable civilian rescue and the nurturing medical care that is *so typical,* he noted, of Huntington Hospital.

Still, he didn't want anyone to know he'd told me this.

I parked my Nova in the lot. The hospital was not on Route 110, as one might expect, but nestled behind it, proving that in Huntington, everything—even health care—played second banana to retail. Halfway to the emergency room I ran back to the car, opened the hatchback, pulled the plastic off a recently dry-cleaned blazer, and put it on to cover the notebook in my rear pocket.

Inside, the receptionist studied her clipboard.

"Is Amalia here?" I asked.

"Amalia Sanchez?"

A banner—"Huntington Hospital Is a Happy Hospital"—fluttered on the white screen behind her. Beyond it, I heard a patient moan. Under the banner, there was a poster:

"Join Us as Our Happy Hospital Celebrates Sir Oliver Cromwell Day at the Huntington Yacht Club."

This didn't sound like a good idea, naming a fund-raiser after one of the major tyrants of the seventeenth century.

"Yes, Mrs. Sanchez," I said, guessing. The PR man, typically, had refused to give me a last name. But how many Amalias could there be at Huntington Hospital?

The woman glared at her clipboard, then peered suspiciously over the rims of her tortoiseshell bifocals as the electronic door behind me swooshed open. Three graying men with ruddy faces glided in together.

"Suffolk County Homicide," one of them said.

"Homicide," agreed the other two.

"Here to interrogate Mrs. Sanchez!" the first detective announced.

Why hadn't any of the cops Mulvaney called told him that the hospital had a murder suspect?

"I'm Amalia's friend," I chirped, even though Leisure Suit had some new dumb rule that we couldn't lie.

The first detective examined me. "Then you speak Spanish, right?"

"Like a native," I lied again as he motioned me to follow.

It had been a tough night for Amalia Sanchez, and she was in no position to be choosy about her friends. The cops, speaking English v-e-r-y s-l-o-w-l-y, told her to tell me everything she wanted them to know.

Reporter heaven. It does happen more than once in a lifetime, even on Long Island.

Amalia grasped my hand in her dark, bony one, as if we'd known each other all our lives, and I thanked Midwood High School for whatever Spanish it might have forced down my throat.

As she spoke, her eyebrows moved with her. They were thick and curly, not tweezed into an expression of surprise, like so many women's.

"Ask her when she threw her boyfriend out the window," ordered the first detective. "Before or after she set the fire?"

"*Mi perrito muerto,*" she wailed quietly.

"*Ay,*" I said, thinking *Oy*. These guys had no idea they were investigating the alleged homicide of a puppy. I thought of Mulvaney, who claimed nobody was smarter than a cop.

"Come se llama el perro?" I asked her. If you wrote about pets, you needed to get their names.

"Dani," she said, wiping her face with a shredded tissue. *"Danielito, mi Daniel. Daniel Ortega Saavedra, el perrito."*

This, I thought to myself, could be a better story than I'd imagined.

"Mi perrito precioso. El mejor perrito del mundo."

The lead detective turned to his boys. "Ain't Danny the name arson gave us?"

"He's a dog," I explained, trying to sound matter-of-fact. It is always best to let cops in on their own mistakes gently.

"Broads always make excuses," the lead detective said.

I shook my head. "As in bow-wow."

The detectives' red faces turned white.

"Daniel was a dog?" the lead detective asked.

"A little one," I said.

I arrived back in the Gloomroom and spotted Mulvaney on the phone miserably asking questions about automobile alarms. He saw me, too, and clicked his tongue in mock scolding. He'd probably heard from Homicide by now. Around us the Non-*Naked* Men typed furiously, their white shirts unbuttoned, their headphones askew.

Fifteen minutes to deadline.

"Fischkin, whattaya got?" A photograph of a red Mazda leaned against Leisure Suit's computer.

"I love it!" he shrieked as I filled him in.

Leisure Suit and dog stories were made for one another.

"I absolutely love it." He rose from his chair and climbed on top of the City Desk Without a City.

Mulvaney, who could giggle like a little boy, was doing just that.

"Stop the presses!' Leisure Suit shouted, stamping his foot perilously close to his computer terminal. Mulvaney's giggles escalated to hysteria.

The only people who actually could stop the presses—the pressmen—were miles away in Garden City, studying the intricacies of publishing with newfangled computers regularly imperiled by excitable editors.

Shaking with delight, Leisure Suit climbed down and told me to write my own budget note.

RONKONKOMA BUREAU

Radical Arson

Liberate Me, the only Alternative Bookstore in Huntington, burned to the ground last night in what police say was a suspicious fire. As flames spread, the bookstore owner roused his second-floor tenant by throwing used Communist Manifestos at her window. She tossed her dog, Daniel Ortega, out the window into the landlord's arms, then jumped herself. Tenant in guarded condition at Huntington Hospital. Landlord and dog missing. All believed to be Nicaraguan revolutionaries, immigration status unknown but probably not good.

At my desk I read the notes I'd scrawled from memory in the hospital parking lot and wrote the real story.

I popped my head up to see Mulvaney standing over me. "Good dog story. Did you call your mother for a quote?"

He had a pencil behind his ear. All he needed was a black visor and he could play himself in *The Front Page*. "My friends at Homicide, though," he added, "are not amused by your deception."

Two minutes to deadline and he was bothering me.

In the end I'd had to tell the detectives I was a *Newsday* reporter.

But they'd given me the quote I needed and told me I had wonderful foreign language skills for someone assigned to Huntington. My little lie, they assured me, didn't concern them nearly as much as the guys in Arson, who'd left the crime scene convinced it was a human, not a dog, tossed from the apartment window. These guys made me look like Gabriel García Márquez.

"Oh, bullshit, Mulvaney," I said. "They thought it was very funny."

I swiveled my chair and started typing.

Mulvaney put his hand on the keyboard. "They found the dog. It wandered back home and the cops took it in for questioning." Leisure Suit stood and surveyed the City Desk Without a City, as if he might climb it again.

Mulvaney was wearing a clean shirt. "You don't even have to give me a piece of the byline." Leisure Suit clapped twice, pulled a leg high.

I made this update "the kicker"—the last sentence—and looked around to see if the Only Female Assistant Editor in Ronkonkoma was in. If she was, she'd make me put the dog's current whereabouts in the lead. That would make the top clunky and ruin the flow of the entire story. But suspense, I suspected, was no longer an attribute the only female assistant editor admired.

"Mulvaney," I said, "the cops tell you anything else about the dog?"

"Yeah, they said it yaps."

The police added that the dog barked merrily, in antici-pation, perhaps, of a reunion with its owner.

I pressed "Send" and waited for questions.

Story sent, I nodded at Mulvaney, who was back on the phone. "You don't want a byline? What do you want?"

He hung up and smiled blue. "The usual."

"Who were you talking to?"

"Northern Ireland."

"Mulvaney," I said, "for me you hung up on an entire country?"

"Isn't a country," he replied. "Or, it shouldn't be."

We drove down to Long Beach and stopped at the 7-Eleven to buy beach towels. Mulvaney claimed he had some in his bungalow, but we'd never find them in the rubble that was supposed to be a floor. It had been warm for a May night but the ocean was freezing, particularly if you weren't wearing anything.

"Did the bookstore owner ever show?" I asked as we dried off.

"Hard to tell. He used a few names."

"A bookstore owner with aliases?"

"Remember the kind of bookstore. And now the broad's gone missing, too."

"Amalia!"

"Yep, your best friend. Walked right out of the hospital. Didn't even collect her puppy."

I pulled the towel off him. "Cops call after I sent the story?"

He nodded and went for my towel. "I don't think they're

really Nicaraguans," he said as I ran out from under the streetlight on the boardwalk.

"Mulvaney," I said, pulling my jeans on, "something better than a fire is going on here." I thought of her face. "She had eyebrows like a woman who did not have time for nonsense."

"You could adopt the mutt."

I kissed him. "Do we really need another dog story?"

Even now, I remember falling in love
with Mulvaney and thinking it wouldn't be necessary for
him to sing to me.

Perhaps, when it comes to this book, I am being inflexible.
Mulvaney is still smart, still handsome, still employed, and
still interesting, even in bed, although I do not want to write
about that.

But he's not asking me to. He says he can be standing up
for most of this.

I'm a writer. This is something I can do for my husband.

CHAPTER 14

Teamwork, Part Two

Fischkin," Leisure Suit said, shaking his head, "I just don't see a story."

The editor's right hand tapped out gibberish on his keyboard. The left linked a chain of paper clips around a sterling silver frame in which he'd put the image of his beloved Mazda. If only Leisure Suit's mind worked as well as his fingers.

"They're raising money *in the name of Oliver Cromwell,*" I repeated.

He nodded. "Yes, it's a mildly interesting gimmick. Historically accurate, too. Did you know that Huntington was settled by people from Cromwell's hometown, Huntingdon with a 'd'?"

He stopped typing but continued linking his paper clips. "Now that I think of it, wasn't Cromwell the founder of the British Royal Navy? Get it? Navy—yacht club."

"He massacred people right and left!"

"War is hell," Leisure Suit agreed.

A Non-*Naked* Man stood and stretched. His shirt stuck to his potbelly. The May heat wave hadn't broken.

"Would you say the same thing about Hitler?" I asked, making a mental note to join the union, now that I had passed the Gloomroom probationary period. "Would you say that he did what he did because war is hell?" Another Non-*Naked* Man pulled a handkerchief from his pocket and wiped his perspiring face.

"I need a weather story," Leisure Suit said. He liked those almost as much as he liked dog stories.

There was a sweaty commotion at the entrance to the Gloomroom: Mulvaney returning from Manhattan. Somehow he'd convinced Leisure Suit that the only way to find out about Long Island car theft was to go into the city. I'd asked him to check while he was there for anything new on the alleged Long Island Nicaraguans.

"Mulvaney," Leisure Suit yelled out, "you got any heat-related crime?"

Mulvaney stomped over to the City Desk Without a City and slammed his notebook so that it barely missed Leisure Suit's hand. "I don't do weather," he said.

"Mulvaney," I said, "you should at least do storms."

Leisure Suit raised his eyebrows. "I hadn't realized you knew Mulvaney so well."

Mulvaney smiled lightning blue at me. "Rain, I understand," he went on. "My ancestors came from rain. They came from a small wet town in the west of Ireland."

Leisure Suit was back on the keyboard. "Where was that?" he asked, staring at his terminal.

"They called it Mulvenna."

I moaned.

"Doesn't exist anymore." Mulvaney looked at me and winked. "Cossacks burned it down."

I shook my head, but he was too delighted with himself to stop. "My relatives had to flee to America on a boat without chocolate."

Leisure Suit looked up from the computer, slid open his desk drawer with a jagged back-and-forth motion, and grabbed another box of paper clips. "They had Cossacks in Ireland?" he asked.

"Yeah," I offered. "They rode in with Oliver Cromwell."

The new box of paper clips spilled out onto the floor. My brown eyes locked into Mulvaney blue. We knew we couldn't laugh, or even smile.

"You didn't know that Oliver Cromwell hired Cossacks?" Mulvaney paused and looked hard at the editor. "Oliver Cromwell and fifty-two Cossacks rode into Mulvenna, Ireland, on a cold, wet morning in 1649 and set the town on fire. His soldiers killed on sight. Within hours, half the town was dead."

The editor bent to pick up his paper clips, but he didn't take his eyes off Mulvaney.

Well, I thought, just because stuff like that happened in my mother's Felshtin didn't mean it never happened in Mulvaney's Mulvenna, or even someplace more factual.

"They herded all the women into a boat," Mulvaney said. "A boat without chocolate. They were sold as slaves in the West Indies. To the Brits!"

Leisure Suit sat still.

"Irish slaves, of course, were worth more because they were white."

"A lot of white women belong to the Huntington Yacht Club," I said.

"Sir Oliver Cromwell Day," Mulvaney agreed. "The Ancient Order of Hibernians is livid—and you know that Irish temper." He put an arm around me, in conspiratorial mode, but he spoke loudly. "Got that from a *Daily News* photographer. Buddy o' mine."

Our editor, I knew, couldn't stand it when a city paper beat him on a Long Island story. This was my chance but I had to act quickly.

"Guess I better write it," I said.

Leisure Suit looked exhausted. "Make it short," he said.

After deadline we invited everyone at *Newsday* to drink with us at the Ground Round. Getting people to drink to excess and spill their guts was at the top of the list of non-sex things Mulvaney and I did best together. Everyone from Ronkonkoma—except Leisure Suit, who didn't drink but should have—squeezed into the bar. It was so crowded the fake Tiffany lamps shook. When we thought the place could hold no more, the Men Who *Did* Write *Naked Came the Stranger* arrived from Garden City to regale us with stories about their days as undercover pornographers.

"Those were better times," they all agreed in unison. "Before newspapers had computers."

Just before midnight, the Only Female Assistant Editor in Ronkonkoma appeared. She threw back a few shots of bourbon and—to the delight of most of us but especially Claire—described what it had been like to work in Chicago and sleep with Mike Royko's best friend.

"He wasn't as good a reporter as Mulvaney," she said. She told Mulvaney that he was the best police reporter in Suffolk County. I was afraid he'd hit her.

"The only police reporter," he said sadly. "Not enough news for two."

After Mulvaney pours wine for me,
he starts to cook. He makes delicious meals, but after he
"cleans up," there is a mess. He says this is because he is "a
complicated human being." When we still worked in
Ronkonkoma, Mulvaney would open cans and call it
"cooking dinner for you." I fell for that, too, but it was also a
trick, a failed attempt to convince me that he himself was as
simple as Chicken Noodle.

CHAPTER 15

Do Lyrics Count?

Mulvaney stomped over to the City Desk Without a City minutes before deadline and plunked down fuzzy black-and-white NYPD photographs of an upside-down luxury automobile. "Guaranteed stolen late this morning from Long Island," he announced. "Southern State to Belt, flipped over during a cop chase in Brooklyn."

Leisure Suit clutched the pictures in his long, lanky fingers.

"Lucky thief," Mulvaney said. "He *strolled* into the cops' arms. Won't need to be wheeled through his perp walk."

The editor held up the photos to the Gloomroom's fluorescent lights, then lowered them, perilously close to the picture of his own Mazda. He tinkered with the cloth buckle of his leisure suit.

"Good wreck shot," he said, putting the pictures aside a bit nervously. "Where'd they steal it *from*?"

Throughout the Gloomroom, we all swiveled our chairs to watch.

"He took it from a newspaper parking lot in Ronkonkoma," Mulvaney said.

A few reporters stood to get a better view.

Leisure Suit's eyes went wide. He peeled a single staple off a long row, pushed the photos aside, squinted at them sideways.

"Ronkonkoma?" he asked.

Mulvaney nodded solemnly.

Leisure Suit picked the photos up again, and when he slammed them down his whole body jerked like a new corpse. From his open desk drawer, he grabbed three boxes of staples and flung them in the general direction of Mulvaney, sending slivers of metal hailing down, making visibility poor. The editor ran into the thick of that storm, hugged himself tight, and let out a small, incomprehensible yelp.

"Mulvaney!" he yelped more coherently. "Mulvaney, you fucking bastard! You had my car stolen!"

Mulvaney smiled his widest blue. "Nah. Must have been that new car-theft ring."

To Mulvaney's complete and utter amazement, this stunt did not further endear him to Leisure Suit. It was, to be blunt, a major setback for his career.

Suddenly he was reined in, banned from Manhattan, ordered

to Babylon instead. His stories ran in the back of the paper and he spent nights at the Ground Round complaining that Leisure Suit couldn't take a joke; that the car had only needed a few "minor" repairs.

"You'd better lay low or you'll have to leave the country," I said.

But with fewer stories to report, Mulvaney was sweeter, and life with him was slower. If I worked late, he went to my cottage and warmed up a can of Campbell's soup. One night he insisted that we go out alone, to a place we knew in Huntington that served good mussels.

His eyes softened and I panicked. He was, as I had always believed, as I should have remembered, a typically deranged Irishman. Mulvaney was going to ask me to marry him! And the romance had been going so well. . . .

Fall had started early. We hung our jackets in a small cloakroom packed with other customers' coats. Months earlier Mulvaney had discovered an old jukebox in that room and the owners had moved it out front. After we got our table he put two quarters in and Rosemary Clooney crooned: *Of sunburns at the shore / nights in Singapore / you might have been a headache / but you never were a bore.*

When the mussels arrived, Mulvaney took one, threw the shell back in his bowl.

"There are still people in Ireland who won't eat these," he said.

I nodded. Months had passed since my Oliver Cromwell story had run upfront, prompting Huntington Hospital to change the name, and the theme, of its fund-raiser. Even longer since Physty the whale had finally made it back to sea.

"Famine food," Mulvaney said. "When there were no potatoes, they dug mussels out of the shoreline."

I wished he'd stop stalling so I could tell him that I was not ready to marry anyone, particularly him.

"I'm leaving Ronkonkoma," he said.

"Mulvaney, did you get a job at the *Times*?"

"Nope, a fellowship to go to Northern Ireland."

"Mulvaney," I said, "fellowships come from universities."

"Yep, got one from St. John's."

I put down my own mussel. What would I do if he asked me to come with him?

"For how long?"

"Could be two years. The school's going to pay me to write stories for *Newsday*. Won't cost the paper a cent."

"When?"

"I'm going next week," he said. "I hope you'll write to me."

I hadn't known you could get food poisoning so quickly, even from shellfish.

All the men before Mulvaney had either walked out on me or stayed and bored me. Mulvaney had seemed to be staying but I wasn't bored. It had never occurred to me that he might be. That wasn't what the song said.

"Mulvaney, you are going to Ireland without me?"

He nodded.

"Good," I said. "Saves me the trouble of dumping you."

I'd never seen blue eyes turn navy before. A shade darker than even midnight. "In a trillion years would you ever go to Ireland? You don't even want to go to Israel, why would you want to go to Ireland?"

I'd write but not to him. Writing to Mulvaney would be almost as big a waste of time as *attempting* to write with Mulvaney around. I could have written a lot more stories if I'd never gone out with him.

He stood. "Would you ever in a trillion years even consider

leaving a job to follow a man? I don't think so. Would you ever quit your job and follow me to another country to *watch me* write stories?"

Why did he think I would go just to watch?

I arrived in the Gloomroom the next day later than usual, as late as I could without risking a full-blown Leisure Suit attack. No way was I going to sit there and wait for Mulvaney to sashay in and start calling every tavern owner in New York who might be harboring an Irish Republican Army fugitive under the sink. Let him sit and wonder where *I* might be.

This plan worked for two days. By the time I got to Ronkonkoma, Mulvaney was either out on assignment or AWOL, probably trying to cover Belfast from Manhattan.

On the third day, Leisure Suit called me at home, insisting that I needed to start coming in earlier. "But not today," he said. In a rare break from tradition, he asked me to start my day on my actual beat instead of in Ronkonkoma.

A Huntington woman had been arrested after shooting her husband. Unfortunately, she didn't kill him.

"Go do the neighborhood!" he commanded. "Come in and dump notes to Mulvaney. You're going out with him, right?"

I put on the first thing I spotted in my huge, empty walk-in closet, a pair of jeans. So what if Mulvaney had told me it was those jeans that drove him over the brink and into the shul. Putting them on was merely coincidence, and it didn't matter, anyway. Now *nothing* would come between me and my Calvins.

"Story any good?" Mulvaney asked as I walked toward his desk.

"The neighbor's taste in men is marginally better than my own," I said, trying not to be swallowed up by blue. I faced the wall but could feel him surveying the jeans.

"Keep your fucking eyes to yourself," I said.

"You kiss your mother with that mouth?" he asked me very quietly.

As he typed the quotes I dictated, Mulvaney told me that the cops shared our suspicion that Amalia Sanchez might not have been who she said she was.

"So what else is new?"

He typed more and asked me if I could help his father get an apartment in a middle-income housing project in Rockaway. The elder Mulvaney had just traded his third wife for the reliable comfort of his barstool at Pier 92, and he'd spotted a government-subsidized building he liked close by.

I couldn't believe Mulvaney was asking me this.

I also couldn't believe that there were three women in the world who would actually marry a Mulvaney.

"Steingut is the landlord. He owes you," Mulvaney said, as if he himself didn't. "It would be a good way to let him make it up to you."

"Your father has a barstool," I said. "Why does he need an apartment, too?"

Those were the last words I spoke to Jim Mulvaney before he left for Belfast.

I'd forgotten about the mussels, forgotten
Rosemary Clooney was there that night, too. This is the peril
in writing a book about your husband. Writing is
remembering.

CHAPTER 16

Thanks for the Memories

Mulvaney sent me a postcard from the Giant's Causeway, an enormous Northern Irish glacial formation. It had been months since he'd left me to cover a minor ethnic dispute that had been raging for about eight hundred years with no solution in sight.

"Write back," Claire urged. "And be nice."

I mailed him a photograph of Mount Rushmore:

Dear Mulvaney:

Here in America, we use our rocks to make heads. You, I imagine, use yours to fill them.

Sincerely,
Barbara Fischkin

All winter I had tried not to read the stories Mulvaney filed from Northern Ireland. I did, though, read other people's stories. I read books about the place, too, and hated myself for all of it. I was sure that those historic troubles only begat more troubles.

In February the *New York Times Sunday Magazine* published a tale about Belfast family life by a reporter who lived with her children near Hampstead Heath in northern London. Minutes after my mother saw it, she suffered a gall bladder attack of epic proportions.

I brought her home from the hospital but she refused to stay in bed and kept asking me how I managed to get dumped by Mulvaney before she had a chance to convert him. My father was no help and Queen Asta made me sneeze. After two long days I needed a break. "I have to go meet a source," I told my mother.

At the liquor store on Utica Avenue, a red-brick hovel with a pink neon sign on its marquee, I went into the small phone booth, closed the folding wooden doors, and took a deep breath. I called Claire but she wasn't home, so I opened my "beatbook," to see if I really could find a source to meet. Leisure Suit, who should have been a dead kindergarten teacher, checked our beatbooks regularly. "Fischkin," he'd told me, "you need more categories."

I turned to my latest category: "More Likely to Have a Story Than the Usual Huntington Stiff," and called Gary Ackerman, a Huntington source who lived in Queens, which explained how he'd made it into that particular section.

He was also a congressman.

"Meet me at Pier 92," he said.

I gulped. "It's not in your district."

"It's my favorite bar." The congressman, I knew, was not a drinker. "I like their steaks," he explained.

•   •

Gary Ackerman lived in Jamaica Estates, Mario Cuomo's old neighborhood, and represented a constituency that stretched from northern Queens to the eastern edge of Huntington and included struggling Dominican immigrants, the last of Long Island's old-money Gold Coasters, and everyone in between. In lieu of trying to make all the members of that hodgepodge happy, Ackerman had joined the Foreign Legion, or the congressional equivalent, the House Foreign Affairs Committee.

Which was why I needed to talk to him or, at the least, humor him. The congressman had deployed his Washington staff to do for me what Mulvaney hadn't, locate the alleged Nicaraguans. If Amalia and the bookstore owner—or even the dog—had committed any really terrific political crimes, it would make the best kind of Huntington story, one that threatened to deflate property values. It might also be my ticket out of *Newsday* to a paper that actually covered Manhattan.

But if I went to Pier 92, I might go nuts first.

I sped over the Gil Hodges bridge into Rockaway, throwing back gin from a bottle in a paper bag and thanking the Jewish God for not shutting down the only liquor store in my parents' section of Flatbush-Midwood-Flatlands. All they'd had at their house was last Passover's Manischewitz, and it was almost spring again. I looked up at the bridge's thick lattice ironwork and then out onto Jamaica Bay and wondered how cold I'd be if I jumped. Just my luck, someone would probably save me. The Rockaway Peninsula was an uneven conglomeration of oceanfront communities, some litter-strewn, others sparkling, but all of them civic-minded in their own way. Dan Tubridy himself had periodically saved drowning middle-aged miscreants and troubled adolescents. I didn't know, though, if he had any experience jumping into the bay to rescue lovelorn, gin-soaked newspaper reporters.

I vowed not to think about going to Pier 92 with Mulvaney during our own Year of Living Dangerously on and around Long Island. This was the post-Mulvaney period of my life. Soon I wouldn't even be calling it that. Besides, there was no law against developing my own bar to hang out in, even if it was in Rockaway.

I did have a source who was a regular.

And I did not hold it against the Real Mulvaney that he had an idiot for a son.

On the rickety dock that served as the outdoor vestibule, a large man wearing green Bermuda shorts in the winter chill, topped with a white shirt and orange suspenders—the colors of the Irish flag—pounced from the swinging kitchen doors to my right. He looked as pleased as a gorilla might if he'd burned down the Bronx Zoo.

"Danny!" I said, and hugged him.

"Welcome back to the finest establishment on the Rockaway Peninsula!" He smiled through his generous red beard and gave me the once-over. I remembered the first time he did that. It was a message to Mulvaney, a signal of approval.

"Did we like South Dakota?" he asked.

The dock was chilly. "South Dakota?"

"Home of Mount Rushmore."

How could I have forgotten that there were no secrets in Mulvaneyland?

"I cut the picture out of an encyclopedia," I said. "He send you postcards, too?"

Dan Tubridy smiled wide. "Nah, I'm only the guy who begged St. John's to pay him to write stories for *Newsday*. Why would I get a postcard?"

If your father's bartender got you a newspaper job, why not a university grant, too?

Inside, Pier 92 was even more glorious than before, newly paneled in soft cedar, the color of first dawn. Behind the polished bar a large picture window looked out on the bay and the bridge that crossed it. The sky was clear and the World Trade Center stood in the distance. Beyond the window was the deck, which now had a movable canopy that looked suspiciously like some Irishman's idea of a chuppah.

Who would have a Jewish wedding at an Irish bar in Rockaway?

Gary Ackerman stood at the bar, eating a steak and french fries and wearing his customary white carnation. Sitting on a stool next to him, nursing a martini, was a man who looked like a Mulvaney who had aged well.

The Real Mulvaney.

Ackerman kissed me. "We're working on the Sandinistas," he promised. "But it would be better if *Newsday* sent *you* to Managua."

I considered, not for the first time, the likelihood of that happening out of Ronkonkoma.

"I used to go out with your son," I said to the Real Mulvaney, hoping he'd like the joke.

"Used to?"

Ackerman shook his head at me and asked the bartender for a doggie bag. "If I want to witness strife, I can go to a Third World country." He kissed me goodbye, put his unfinished meal, plate and all, in the bag, and hurried out the door.

I ordered a gin and tonic. Mulvaney's father said he still needed a place to live.

"Tell me something," I asked. "If your buddy is a congressman, why do you need me to ask a former assemblyman to get you an apartment?"

"Specialization," explained the father. "You are familiar with Gary's expertise in foreign affairs?"

I nodded.

"And you've probably guessed my son will someday need help getting out of a foreign prison."

I imagined Mulvaney locked up in a faraway hellhole, which improved my mood.

"So why waste that chit on an apartment?"

I said I would call Stanley Steingut.

The Real Mulvaney. More real than his son? The thought made me shudder.

Driving back on Flatbush Avenue, I reached for the bag on the floor and took another slug of gin. I had to be honest with myself. I was never getting to Manhattan. Even if the city papers would hire me, I didn't want to go to any of them. I wasn't a *Times* type, never had been, and the *Daily News* was, now, almost as bad as the *Post*. Then there was *Newsday,* a pretty good paper that refused to write about Manhattan. *Newsday* covered foreign countries better than Times Square, even if its international operation was run out of Garden City by a potbellied editor who wore a safari suit instead of one made for leisure.

As much as I hated to give politicians credit for anything, Gary Ackerman had a point. I needed to find a way to convince *Newsday* to send me out of the country.

Did I think I could do this without the help of Mulvaney?

Or his father's bartender?

You bet I did.

As I remember more, I consider dumping this project. I wonder why I ever thought it would work.

Mulvaney, though, continues to have a great time standing over me while I write. He says when I'm finished I can do a sequel.

"And another after that. All we ever need is the next story."

The last thing I want to be is my husband's serial biographer.

He has a problem, though.

Not enough sex.

"I thought you said I didn't have to write that?"

Sex not required. The oldest line in the world.

"This book just isn't hot enough," Mulvaney says.

"Maybe later," I murmur.

Women have their own lines.

ACT TWO

CHAPTER 17

Chaim Who?

My mother still liked to call me at work.

"I love Paris in the springtime," she crooned, off-key. "And spring is almost over."

True. And I was still in Ronkonkoma.

Leisure Suit appeared at my desk, shot a rubber band in my face, and skipped off. He'd been gone for days at a Message Pending Conference for newspaper editors. But they'd let him come back, proof that new technology could be unreliable.

"Mother, I'm on deadline." I hung up and went back to my story about a Huntington lawyers' club that wouldn't let women join.

She called back. "Our flight's in two days."

What was she talking about?

"You always said you wanted to see Paris."

I must have neglected to mention that I did not want to see it with her.

"Your father won't come with me. The doctor says I can't travel alone."

I hung up for a second time.

The phone rang. "Asta's booked in a kennel."

This *was* serious.

"Paris?" I said. "The only place *you've* ever wanted to go is Israel."

"I found cousins from Felshtin in Paris."

"I thought they only went to Brooklyn and Argentina?"

"These are the Bolsheviks. And soon they will all be dead."

Leisure Suit stood, spread his arms wide, and gazed up at the rotting ceiling, as if he expected my story to fall like manna from heaven.

And I preferred this to the Louvre?

"Mother," I said. "I'll go."

She stood in the terminal waving my ticket and pointing furiously at the clock. I had not been on time for anything since I'd moved to Long Island. My mother's head—she shook that now, too—was adorned with a pink turban. This, I hoped, was nothing worse than her latest fashion statement. Healthy people had stopped wearing those in the sixties.

"I have carry-on," I told her. I could buy more clothes in Paris. Everything else was in my knapsack.

My mother eyed it suspiciously.

"I even have a sweater," I said.

"I hope it's a heavy one." My mother believed that unseasonable cold waves threatened the very survival of the human race.

She lifted her own orange and green tote and loped three strides like an aboriginal cartoon character, stopped, took a breath, adjusted her turban, checked my whereabouts, and loped again. I jogged behind her, reassured. She might not be a prima ballerina but she was as vigorous as any woman her age, if not more so. At the Air France gate she took her place behind a noisy American couple who blamed each other for being late. Didn't anyone have a good romance anymore?

We sat in silence as the plane took off. My mother read an in-flight magazine article on Samuel Beckett, who lived in Paris. Well, they did have Theater of the Absurd in common. Finished, she reclined her seat, put her own multicolored sweater over her shoulders, closed her eyes, and snored gently.

At the Ground Round, just hours earlier, Claire and I had chugged Long Island Iced Teas, a new drink which I was convinced they made by mixing a shot from every bottle in the house. Claire had just been named the Second Female Assistant Editor in Ronkonkoma, a dubious honor but one that, she'd insisted, required a celebration. As we drank, we stared at the fake Tiffany lamps and discussed whether French movies overrated the romantic proclivities of French men.

"I'll find out," I had promised her.

In return Claire promised me that she would make up a good excuse to tell Leisure Suit, who did not know I was leaving the country, not to mention Suffolk County. I hadn't even been able to get the accountants to go for this one.

"Get very drunk," she'd advised, ordering another round. "So you can forget this for a few days—and ignore your mother." It occurred to me that I needed to drink even more now than I had when Mulvaney was around, like an old Irish fishwife left on her own.

The captain announced we would have a forty-minute layover, somewhere I'd never heard of. But it sounded English. A second-tier airport, no doubt, but still likely to have a pub. I nodded off listening to a mix of accents and languages—French, more soothing than I'd expected, American, British, maybe Scottish—and slept for hours.

"Aldergrove," the loudspeaker cackled. "We'll be landing in Aldergrove Airport in ten minutes."

"Now, where is that?" I asked my mother, suddenly awake herself.

"I have no idea," she said, her voice clipped. The plane dove deeper.

The blond woman in front of us turned. "Ach aye," she said, unable to contain her excitement. "It's Belfast. Best city in the whole bloody world."

The words hit me like a monster hangover. They hit me like food poisoning from a rotting mussel. No, rotting was too sweet. They hit me like a mussel that had calcified over centuries, sitting in the midst of a war no one could end.

I glared at my mother. "Why don't you just deliver me back to the Cossacks?"

"Cossacks don't bring people chocolates, dear," she replied, as if this was a cogent argument.

"Mother!" I shouted. "He's not even Jewish!"

"Shh!" said the Belfast woman.

My mother adjusted her turban. "We are on this flight because I got a good deal, which wasn't easy at the last minute. You should remember, though, that people do convert."

"Mother," I hissed, trying to restrain a violent urge. "He could become the Chief Rabbi of Israel and I wouldn't go near him."

"That's because you don't like Jewish men. If you'd only be a little more reasonable."

I spotted green fields. The plane dove harder. We'd be down any minute.

"I'd like to see Belfast someday, though," my mother said.

"Why would you ever want to see Belfast?"

The woman in front of us turned and glared through the space between the seats. "Greatest city in the world."

"Chaim Herzog," my mother said as we bumped on the ground.

"Chaim who?"

"Herzog! The President of Israel. Shame on you for not knowing he was born in Belfast."

I doubted that was true. "Fine," I said. "You can go to Belfast on your own time. We are not getting off this plane."

"We could buy you an Aran sweater in Aldergrove. Warmest sweaters in the world."

"Ach aye," agreed the woman in front.

"No way," I said.

And I said it loud.

As we taxied in, my mother began to wheeze. The sounds started delicately but built quickly, to an intensity she usually reserved for the B'nai Israel Board of Trustees. Passengers turned, horrified. The woman in front of us stood, handed my mother a can of Coke, and spoke soothingly, in a Scottish accent that I now knew wasn't Scottish at all but Northern Irish.

The flight attendant appeared. "Your mother will have to disembark."

The object of her concern was now making sounds unknown to the human experience.

"She's faking," I said. People got thrown off planes because they had guns, knives, or too much to drink. Not for bogus coughs.

"Yew must hate yer mum," the woman in front said.

"I am sorry," the flight attendant replied stiffly. "We cannot chance bringing an American plague to Paris."

"You should have thought of that before you sold my mother a ticket."

The woman in front sniffed and retrieved her bag from the overhead compartment. A few of the other passengers stood to pull down their carry-ons and glare at me. "Aye, that's why Belfast is the best place to live in the whole bloody world," a woman closer to the door chimed in. "People in Belfast do not hate their mummies."

Yeah, I thought, they only hate each other's mummies.

My wheezing mother stood, patted her turban, and through the noise beckoned me with her hand.

"Have fun, Mother," I said. "I am not going with you."

She walked down the aisle, still wheezing. A second flight attendant wrapped my mother's arm around her shoulder and helped her out the door.

I sighed with relief. Until I realized my mother had my knapsack.

Mulvaney says not to worry. He'll help me write sex. For inspiration he suggests I read the screenplay he is in the midst of writing: *The Jim Mulvaney Story*.

"The whole thing is sex," he says, his chest puffed like a Paperboy without a clue.

I find this an extraordinary comment, coming from a man who thinks he's Henry Miller based on one past literary foray. Years ago, inspired by something the Non-*Naked* Men did on Message Pending, Mulvaney tried to write a dirty book himself.

"Was it good for you?" he'd asked, after I'd read it.

"Mulvaney," I'd said, "have you ever *had* sex?"

CHAPTER 18

Felshtin

In Aldergrove Airport, I ran smack into a cop and banged my hip against something hard, a shining silver pistol.

"Whoa, darlin'."

"I lost my mother, an old American lady," I said breathlessly.

"Sorry for your troubles, darlin'. Are you from New York? Have me a cousin in Queens."

I scanned the departure board, noticed there was a flight to Bordeaux, if I couldn't get back on the Paris plane. Then, in the distance, I spotted my mother loping through a contingent of British soldiers, her health suddenly restored.

"That's her!" I said to the Royal Ulster Constable. "Shoot!"

"Couldn't shoot yer mum, dear."

She'd made it to the exit. I ran past the soldiers and outside, in time to see her wave down a bus. I caught up to it as it pulled away and banged hard on the doors. "Promptness is a virtue," the driver said, pointing to his schedule and motioning me on board.

She sat alone in front of a man wearing a tweed cap and, for no apparent reason, sunglasses, tinted light blue like a sunny sky. Outside it drizzled. "Mother, where's my knapsack?" I demanded. My passport was in it; my wallet, too.

"What knapsack, dear?"

"Mother!"

She smiled and, ceremoniously, unwrapped her turban, draping her shoulders in a stole of pink cloth until she got to the layer that had a photograph stuck to it.

I saw it and yelped.

Mulvaney in Belfast. Mulvaney in Belfast perched in my mother's turban. Typical Mulvaney.

"Didn't want to lose this," my mother said, pulling the photograph off. "Directions are on the back. In case I forget them." I tried to grab it but she held tight.

"We want our knapsack back, don't we, dear? Doesn't he look well?"

He'd grown a beard. It didn't look bad. I swallowed. My mother took off the rest of her turban and stuffed it in her bag. In the Gloomroom they said Mulvaney had rented a room from an IRA family. That was how he found his stories now. He lived with people who set off bombs.

"How did you get that?" I asked.

"How do you think?"

My head pounded. Claire had been in on this, too.

The airport road was worse than the L.I.E., and every few miles British soldiers stopped the bus and asked more questions than a *Washington Post* reporter in an underground garage. After the third stop my mother pulled out a paperback: *Too Long a Sacrifice*. One of the best books about the Irish troubles. If only the title didn't remind me of my former romance.

"The writer seems to have survived being the product of a mixed marriage," my mother said, trying to make conversation.

I remained sullen. "It's not a mixed marriage if both people celebrate Christmas."

The man behind us chuckled through his newspaper. I stood and peered over it to examine him.

Far as I knew, Van Morrison was Northern Ireland's only celebrity.

"Are you a rock star?" I asked.

He put down the paper—a local rag called *The Newsletter*—and looked at me through those sky-blue lenses. "Sorry to disappoint yew, darlin'."

"The duality of this writer's upbringing seems to have made him a brilliant observer," my mother continued, making me wonder what had happened to the woman who used to consider Erma Bombeck a sage.

Outside, the clouds hung stagnant and stubborn, as if they could refuse to mature and might never release the inevitable shower. The next contingent of soldiers stopped the bus and ordered us all off. "Might be a bomb," one of them reported dully. "IRA, you know."

"What a bother!" the man in sunglasses said.

Great, I thought. I am going to get killed running after a man who dumped me. And it's going to be my mother's fault.

We got off with the other passengers and stood a distance down the road while the soldiers searched the inside racks and luggage compartment. Each time the bus shook, I expected it to explode.

My mother, though, did not flinch. Not even when the soldiers took off a large, neatly wrapped package and threw it down the hill.

In the winter of 1919, the Cossacks rode into Felshtin.

"One child to one adult," my grandfather ordered. He sent my mother, the eldest of his three little ones, to hide with her bachelor uncle in the Council House.

Then the Cossacks set the Council House on fire.

My mother, choking but determined, slid through her falling neighbors and pushed her way out the door. She ran, alone, for what seemed like hours, into the snowy countryside, to the places where no Jews lived.

When she could run no longer, she stopped at a haystack, made herself a hole, jumped inside. Throughout the night she listened as the Cossacks—who had just murdered her uncle and hundreds more—rode their horses over her.

In the morning my six-year-old mother climbed out of the hay and ran again, this time to a nearby cottage. She knew that if the people who lived there let her in they could be killed themselves.

"I am the watchmaker's daughter," she said.

Back in the village, my grandfather, hiding with his family in an attic, roused his two younger children and told them they would never see their sister again. He watched, helpless, as my grandmother's grief spiraled until she could not speak through her screams.

Later, searching through mounds of corpses, he found his dead brother and steeled himself to keep looking.

A farmer pulled him away. "I have your daughter," he said. "She is alive."

And so my grandfather became the first person, but far from the last, to marvel at my mother's durability.

Finished, the soldiers sent us back to the bus. I asked my mother, again, for my knapsack.

"Negotiate!" she ordered.

I considered my options. Claire would refuse to wire money. My father would insist on asking my mother. I could try the American consulate. . . .

Was there a foreign officer in the world who would get this?

I looked behind me and realized that the man in sunglasses had disappeared.

"Mother," I said, knowing this was a mistake, "I will say hello to Mulvaney. Then you will give me my stuff and we will go back to the airport."

"Done!" she agreed, sounding much too happy about it.

Gaelic graffiti covered the Belfast train station, resembling hieroglyphics more than it did any modern language.

Tiocfidh Ar La

The black letters obliterated an advertisement for Cadbury chocolates. Under it, as if mandated by a tourist board in exile, a translation:

Our day will come.

With my mother in the lead, we walked past a group of teenagers, young, angry denizens of a war zone, their heads shaved, their pants, noses, and eyebrows adorned with metal spikes. Beyond them a caravan of London-style taxis, large, black, and funereal, lined up alongside dour passengers. The city appeared bare and fractured, just the kind of place that bred good stories. Any other city in the world that looked like this and I might consider staying.

I followed my mother onto the taxi line.

"Felons Club," she said in undeniable Brooklynese. The people behind us gasped.

What the hell, I wondered, was the Felons Club?

The driver said he couldn't take us there.

Thank God.

"Ach, yewr on the Protestant line," a woman scolded. "The Catholic taxis go over there." She pointed across the road to another line of cars that looked exactly the same. "Yew can tell they are Catholic taxis because they are dirty. Protestant taxis are clean."

"We're not Catholic, we're Jewish," my mother called back as I ran after her.

Outside the Felons Club in West Belfast, we stood in front of a booth with a bulletproof window, separating us from a room we could not see but which my mother, in a stage whisper, insisted contained both Mulvaney and the glitterati of the *Provisional* Irish Republican Army.

Provos. These were not old men congratulating themselves over the Easter Uprising of 1916. "Ever committed a crime?" the man behind the booth asked gravely.

"Of course not!" my mother insisted.

"Canna let yew in."

At last. A helpful Irishman.

"We can't get in *unless* we've committed a crime?" my mother asked.

The man nodded sadly. "Why dew yew think we call it the Felons Club, darlin'?"

My mother threw back her head—it would have been a better gesture if she'd left on her turban—and shook it at the sky. Then she looked straight ahead, hard. "This is no way to run a hospitality business," she informed the gatekeeper.

"Sorry, missus."

"Besides," my mother continued, "we know Jim Mulvaney."

"Jimmy Mulvenna's dead," he said gravely.

"No!" I cried out.

"Not since yesterday?" my mother asked.

"Years ago," the man said. I took a breath.

"This is a different one," my mother said.

"Ach, there'll never be another Jimmy Mulvenna."

"Mother," I said, "time for my passport!"

"You have to say hello." She turned back to the man in the booth. "What if we know a criminal?"

He nodded.

"My husband went to jail for gambling," she offered.

He looked at her as if she was trying to pay a king's ransom with pennies. Or pence.

"It would have to be a political crime," the man in the booth noted.

A few years earlier, according to my reading, IRA prisoners

had fought a long, grotesque battle to win concessions to distinguish themselves from the general riffraff, otherwise known as "ordinary, decent criminals."

"No *daysent* criminals," he said. "No wee ordinary ones either."

My mother looked uncharacteristically thoughtful. "*My* husband," she said, "was a prisoner of the Brooklyn Democrats."

"What makes you think *you* can write sex?" my husband demands. "You can't even get us back into bed."

"Just watch," I say.

Sex for Siding

It is a late summer afternoon at a backyard party. The barbeque is raging, flip-flops are strolling in from the beach, and the conversation has reached that fevered, intellectual pitch that is such a signature of the suburbs.

"How's your new house?" someone asks me. Mulvaney is two hours late and this puts me in a reckless mood. "My new house? The one that looks like a Walker Evans photograph?" I reply, confident that no one will know what I mean.

"Yeah."

"I told Mulvaney that if he doesn't fix it up soon, I am going to have an affair with a contractor."

With that, a man turns around.

"Funny," he says, "I'm a contractor."

Quickly, I examine him. He is dark, lanky, and tanned. I wonder if I could be attracted to anyone so conventionally good-looking.

"You're a contractor," I say. "What a coincidence."

"Let Us Now Praise Famous Men," he replies.

There has to be something very wrong with this man.

He looks, with appreciation, at a leg sticking out of the slit of my summer skirt. I am always impressed when men get past the breasts. His eyes, I notice, are green, which would be my downfall if blue eyes did not exist.

Mulvaney is two hours late and it is not as if he is at home painting the kitchen.

"Where do you live?" he asks.

I tell him. "It's the one that needs work," I say.

"Funny," he says, again. "Tomorrow I'm putting a new front on the house across the street from yours."

His eyes twinkle. A man like this could make a woman forget all the bad things she once thought about aluminum siding.

I must have been insane not to see its potential.

CHAPTER 19

Mother's Night

The Felons Club smelled of mildew and its walls were painted the color of olives. So much for kelly green. Swirling pastels danced on a worn carpet that ended at a patch of linoleum—and at a bar packed for lunch.

Mulvaney handed a drink to a woman with curly red hair so long it reached beyond her small waist. She wore a black sweater that made her seem concave, but she had delicate arms, a small nose, porcelain skin. Mulvaney took a strand of that red hair in his hand and playfully shook it up and down.

A souped-up jukebox played "Four Green Fields."

My mother told me she had to go to the bathroom. "Nice

carpeting," she commented as she loped away, swaying to the rebel music.

Slowly he walked over, smiling, taking a slug of stout. "You look great," he whispered in my ear.

And why shouldn't I? Running through an armed airport and riding in an exploding bus is supposed to be good for your skin.

Not to mention your hair.

"Who's that?" I asked. It was not what I had meant to say.

He took a step back. "Marsha McCain. California broad. Fell in love with some IRA guy."

"Just what the world needs, another misguided West Coast idealist."

His new brown beard moved closer to my face. A flash of blue followed. I attempted to ignore it.

This, I reminded myself, was Jim Mulvaney and there was every chance in the world that he had engineered a trans-atlantic quasi-kidnapping not because he loved me or missed me but simply because he knew he could pull it off.

He did not love me any more than he had loved Leisure Suit's Mazda.

"I'm not staying," I said. My hand found its way around his pint glass and I had a long sip.

A shriek filled the room.

"Jim Mulvaney!" my mother exclaimed. "Would you look at us, here, in enemy territory!"

As Mulvaney kissed her on the cheek, the thugs at the closest table turned to glare.

He put his arm around me. I took it off.

"No passport until you meet Mulvaney's friends!" My mother, who'd never made a deal she couldn't modify, shook a long red fingernail at me.

With an extended open palm, Mulvaney steered us toward two men at a round solitary table on the edge of the room, their backs hard against the wall.

One stood. He wore a ratty sweater; a thick black beard obscured his face. So Mulvaney was in fashion.

"Pleased to meet you," he said, taking my hand.

"I'm on the next plane to Paris."

"A pity."

I looked again.

"Gerry Adams," he explained.

Terrific. Thanks to Mulvaney, and my mother, I'd just shaken hands with the commander of the Irish Republican Army.

Not that he admitted to it. He was Irish. Why would he?

"I admire your organizing skills," I told Gerry Adams stiffly.

He was, I knew, now portraying himself as merely a peace-loving politician.

"And *we* all appreciated your eloquent condemnation of Oliver Cromwell Day," he replied.

Double terrific. Mulvaney had twisted my story, turned it into Provo propaganda. He'd probably told them it was all his idea, too.

I nodded in the direction of Thug Number Two. "Gerry Adams's PR man?"

"Yep," Mulvaney replied, pleased as punch.

Danny Morrison, in a leather jacket, was boyish and hand-some. He also looked familiar.

"Director of Public Relations, Sinn Fein," he said, waving from his seat.

I waved back. "You do know how Mulvaney feels about PR men?"

Morrison winked, pulled out a chair for my mother. "Yer man Mulvaney's a troublemaker," he said.

Even the IRA thought so.

A waitress came. Drinking seemed to be my only option, so I ordered a gin and tonic. My mother asked for an apricot sour, which was what she drank at bar mitzvahs, weddings, and other shul events, except for Las Vegas Saturday Nite, which had been brazenly reinstated as "Take a Chance on Saturday Nite"—and at which no alcohol was served. The waitress grimaced at Danny Morrison, as if my mother was all his fault.

"You don't have apricot sours in Belfast?" my mother asked, amazed.

Morrison nodded toward the bartender. "Tell yer man to mix blackberry brandy with vodka." He turned back to my mother. "Made from *Israeli* blackberries."

I made a mental note to enlighten my mother about the IRA's ties to the PLO. They were also hooked up with Basque separatists, the worst of the Sandinistas, Fidel Castro, and everyone else in the world who had ever contemplated bombing as a civic duty.

"Every war should have a PR man like you," I said coolly.

Morrison winked at me. "Every war should have a wee bottle of apricot brandy." He reached into the lapel pocket of his tweed jacket, pulled out a matching cap, and held it open like a mock beggar. A pair of sunglasses with sky-blue lenses rested inside. He put them on, then nodded, as a fellow bus passenger might.

So it had been a Morrison, only not Van.

•   •

Half an hour and two blackberry vodkas later, my mother swore that Gerry Adams and Danny Morrison were two of the nicest men she'd ever met.

"She liked the Irgun, too," I informed them.

Mulvaney's blue eyes stayed calm. Lunchtime in Belfast and he was already drunk?

My mother now clucked over Project Children, Northern Ireland's answer to the Fresh Air Fund.

"I could take a *wee* Belfast girl," she offered. Her Irish accent was dreadful. "For a summer of peace in Brooklyn."

"Just keep the child away from Las Vegas Saturday Nite," I said.

"Leave your mother alone," Mulvaney said softly. "Everyone makes up for being a survivor in their own particular way."

What, I wondered, had Belfast done to him?

The other thing that surprised me, although it shouldn't have, was that my mother was telling Danny Morrison that she had once saved her own life by hiding in a haystack.

Mulvaney leaned toward me. "Can you buy an ArmaLite with Israeli bonds?"

"Do not," I warned him, "try to sweet-talk me."

Suddenly, a hand landed on my shoulder. It was plump, female, and sported a thick bracelet with a large golden charm, an antique-looking insignia: hands, a heart, and a crown melded together.

A crown at the Felons Club?

"Hower yew?" A large woman in a yellowed Aran sweater, her wild hair dyed three shades of blond, bent down and smacked a wet kiss on my cheek. "I'm Suzie McBreeze, Jim

Mulvenna's landlady." So this was her. I'd heard, too, that she had a husband on the run and a rap sheet of her own.

Two more Aran-sweatered women accompanied her. One, small and mousy, greeted us with a giggle and sat. She probably killed people from *behind* the scenes.

"Me name's Joan Collins," said the other, her wrinkled face glowing over the announcement. "Just like yer woman on *Dinnn-est-teee*." Gerry Adams nodded at her in a way that made me sure they had known each other for years.

"Welcome to Mother's Night!" Suzie said, plopping down next to me. Between her legs she held a narrow canvas bag. "Three glasses of tonic water," she demanded from the waitress. "With three limes. Ach, it's hot as a Peeler station in here."

"Peeler?" I said, trying not to sound interested.

"Cops," Mulvaney said. "A guy named Peel was the first Brit police chief. Well, the first real one, anyway..."

Suzie removed her Aran sweater to reveal a white ruffled blouse, which—when it had been in style twenty years ago—was called a Lizzie, after Elizabeth Taylor. Her yellowed bra peeked out from behind cracked buttons.

I caught a glimpse of Marsha McCain at the next table.

Mulvaney moved his hand up my leg. I shook him off and kicked him hard in the shins. Gently, he kicked me back.

"Tell me again?" I asked Suzie. "What night?"

"Mother's Night!"

"What," I asked, "does one do on Mother's Night?"

"Ach aye," she said. "What does it look like we're doing?"
The three tonics arrived. "Sobering up?" I asked.

"Just watch."

She unzipped her canvas bag. A large bottle of gin with a

spout top sat securely inside it. Carefully, Suzie put her glass of tonic on the floor under the table and, without taking the gin out of its bag, poured herself a healthy shot.

"Tumblers, girls!" she said to her two friends.

I looked at Danny Morrison.

"It's okay. They're heroines of the revolution."

"Mother's Night," Suzie repeated with a wide grin.

"It's barely afternoon," I said, suddenly remembering that. Mulvaney's hand scooted up my leg again. I banged my knees shut, hard.

"We start early."

Stevie Wonder blared through the Felons Club. Suzie and her friends dabbed their eyes, sipped their contraband gin, and sang to their absent men. . . .

"*I just called to say I love you . . .*"

My mother put her hand on Suzie's shoulder. Suzie put her own hand on top of it and left it there till the song finished.

"Yer Jewis, right?" Suzie asked, leaving out the final "h," as if she was speaking some backward, drunken, Belfast version of Cockney.

My mother nodded. "Israeli blackberries," she said, cheerfully holding up her glass.

"Are yew a Catholic Jew or a Protestant Jew?"

"A Catholic Jew," my mother said, not missing a beat.

"Chaim Herzog was from Belfast," Suzie said.

Sure he was.

"Wasn't he a Protestant Jew?" my mother asked.

"Ach aye," Suzie said sadly, turning to me. "And yer man's coming here. State visit."

Sounded like a non-story to me.

• •

I was jarred out of Israel in Belfast by the sound of Mulvaney asking Danny Morrison about Nicaragua. I glared at him. I did not need his help on the Sandinista dog story anymore. Nor would I take it.

Nor should he dare to steal it.

Like a scolded child, he made an intercontinental detour, back across the Atlantic. "Can you get me onto the Shankill?" he asked. Now he was beyond drunk. The Shankill Road was the bastion of the Ulster Defense Association, Protestant paramilitaries and sworn enemies of the IRA.

But Danny Morrison raised a pint of lager and said that if Mulvaney wrote a story from the Shankill it would prove that he was a fair journalist, not merely a Provo drinking buddy, even if that was exactly what he appeared to be at the moment.

"We'll introduce yew to Paisley." The Reverend Ian Paisley, the most prominent of Protestant extremists, was large and feral, an instigator who portrayed himself as an earnest preacher.

Could this get worse?

I didn't have to wait long for the answer. "A new couch, even new upholstery, is not always the only solution." My head bounced back to my mother. She was giving the Provisional IRA home-decorating advice.

Suzie dove down to fill her cup with more gin. "It started as a wee hole in the seat and now it's the fookin' Grand Canyon. There's these wee bits of stuffing..."

"I can send you some inexpensive slipcovers from Brooklyn," my mother offered.

"Aye, that would be brilliant," Suzie said.

"In an interesting print to highlight the rest of your décor," my mother added.

Mulvaney was next at the jukebox. *"Sunburns at the shore / nights in Singapore / you might have been a headache / but you never were a bore."*

Only the Bob Hope version, but bad enough.

"Would you like to dance?" he asked me, returning to the table.

We never had.

"If I cared," I told him, "I would hate this song."

"You don't listen to lyrics."

"Mulvaney," I said, "I really do not know what I am doing here. First you leave me. Then you drag me back, practically by my hair."

"I got here and realized I was wrong——"

"I'll dance with you, Jim."

Who else but my mother would interrupt my best moment?

When they had finished, my mother congratulated Mulvaney on being the only man on earth who danced worse than her husband. Then she announced she was leaving for the Europa Hotel.

I'd read about that place, too. It had been bombed so many times it made the airport buses look like coach tours to Shangri-la. If my mother was nostalgic for her pogrom, the Europa was the place to be.

I got up, too.

"I don't have a reservation for you," she said.

"Fine. I'm going to the airport."

"You don't have a passport."

"I'll call my editor. He'll know someone."

This, I realized, was highly unlikely. The State Department did not maintain a satellite office in Ronkonkoma.

Danny Morrison walked to my side of the table and closed his hand over mine. Not too tight but tight enough. "The airport is closed."

"It's the middle of the day."

"They've had a bomb scare."

Did they realize this was an epidemic?

His hand didn't move.

"How do you know that?"

"How do you think he knows that?" Mulvaney said.

Suddenly more thugs appeared behind my mother. Morrison had ensured this would run as smoothly as an armed assault on Buckingham Palace. As they escorted her out, she told them her ideas for a new Project Children brochure. "A scene from *Oliver Twist* might work," she mused. "Don't forget to wear your sweater!" she called back to me as they moved en masse through the doorway.

"That's it," I said, trying to pull out from the PR man's grasp.

With one hand Morrison slipped off his leather jacket. Around his shoulder was a holster with a black gun that looked like a sharpened piece of coal.

I looked at Mulvaney. "Are you absolutely nuts?" I said. "You're going to have your friend shoot me?"

Danny Morrison chuckled and shook his head. "Wouldn't be very good for me public relations to shoot the press, now would it?" he said, loosening his grip.

"You can leave," Mulvaney said. "But I wish you wouldn't."

Sex for Siding (continued)

My contractor shows up in the morning, as promised. I look out from one of our windows, which are not Andersen windows but could and should be, and reexamine his long, muscular arms, his tan, and, yes, his siding.

I no longer care what he reads.

The fact that he is not, literally, my contractor, that he still belongs to the neighbors, makes him all the more intriguing.

Still, I stay inside. Best not to have him see me like this, in a house with old windows and yellow wooden shingles that should be torn down.

Or replaced with something better.

I can't help watching him, though. Every now and then he looks across at our house.

As luck would have it, a Federal Express truck arrives with a package for my husband, which I open quickly. Screenplay: The Foundations of Screenwriting *by Syd Field. Until now, he has been working without the benefit of a manual.*

Didn't I tell you he was brave?

I ponder whether to give it to him or not but I am interrupted by the contractor, who waves, then turns back to his aluminum siding. He wears a tight white T-shirt, blue jeans that are even tighter.

"It's a manual," I say, holding up the book.

"Don't need one," the contractor replies.

A cigarette dangles from his lower lip. He turns and hangs a narrow piece of trim along the edge of the roof. It looks like a Home Depot take on nineteenth-century gingerbread.

"Would you like to learn how to do this?" he asks, without turning from his work.

I go upstairs and deliver Syd Field to Mulvaney. He cracks it open as if it is a case of Irish whiskey. Then he shuts it.

CHAPTER 20

Belfast: The Connoisseur's Tour

Marsha McCain, the red-haired California girl gone Provo, stopped me at the bulletproof booth. "Drinking beer makes women crazy," she said. "And fat."

"I drink gin," I told her. "Lucky me."

I walked out into the murky dusk of the Falls Road, the beleaguered main thoroughfare of West Belfast.

I was supposed to be on the Champs Élysée.

Mulvaney drove up to the curb behind the wheel of a vintage, oversized silver Thunderbird, a car that belonged in Northern Ireland as much as I did. I had agreed to take a quick tour of West Belfast, after concluding that my other choice was to spend the rest of my life inside the Felons Club.

He screeched to a stop, rolled down the window.

"Nice car," I said.

"I got tired of trying to find a Catholic taxi," he replied as he got out the wrong door.

Only Mulvaney would find a quintessentially American car that had a steering wheel on the British side.

We drove and I examined the sights: shops with metal grates pulled halfway down and the occasional virulently anti-British mural, including one of terrified, and terrifying, women that said "Stop the Strip Searches!"

"So which one of those Felons Club charmers was California girl's loverboy?"

"He's in prison," Mulvaney said, *very* matter-of-fact.

I felt myself frowning.

"She's a great story," he offered.

Did he think I'd fall for that? Interview someone, then sleep with her *after* the story runs. Oldest reporter's trick in the book.

She, though, looked dumb enough . . .

"She must be lonely," I said.

"Not interested."

"And why is that?"

He stopped, smiled blue. "The Provos would kill me."

Jim Mulvaney, Master of the Squandered Opportunity.

He put his foot to the gas. With a screech, he swerved left off the Falls Road and stopped short between two looming Celtic crosses.

"IRA Cemetery," he reported.

"Mulvaney," I said, "you are doomed to be a Long Islander."

"Why's that?"

"You drive everywhere."

Suddenly he took off again, flying past ornate tombstones. I leaned against duct tape, a feature of all Mulvaney vehicles, apparently, and hoped it would hold. He screeched to another stop, alongside a black vase stuffed with dying red carnations and daffodils and got out.

"You gotta see this," he said, motioning me to join him.

What are my choices? I thought.

"Read it!" Mulvaney insisted.

I moved closer to the flower pot tombstone. "Oh God, Mulvaney!"

"Great, huh?"

The gold letters said JIM MULVENNA. His blue eyes looked skyward, and that gave me the jitters. The air had an odd, familiar feel to it. Could this be what was wrong with Mulvaney? That he was a ghost who'd returned to the scene of his former life?

I read out loud from the base: " 'Our dear son, killed in action' . . ."

"Yeah, he got hunted down in the woods."

Guerrilla warfare.

"Did he deserve it? He must have done something."

"They've all done something. The question is, what was done to them to make them do it? What made their fathers do what they did? In the middle of the day the streets are filled with men. Catholic men. You could spend a lot of time counting the factories here that won't hire Catholics. Counting the sons in trouble, too . . ."

I stood there between the two Jim Mulvaneys—one doomed, the other potentially so—and imagined I was stuck in a bad country-western song brought to America by who else? The Irish. Rain clouds dotted the black sky and my teeth chattered.

He took my head in his hands and kissed me quickly on the mouth, the way he had done that first time when I had a flat tire outside Taco Bell.

"Don't do it again," I said.

"I was just about to tell you how happy I am that you are here."

"We're in a cemetery, Mulvaney!"

He bent down and cleared a dead flower from Jim Mulvenna's grave.

"And do not be glad that I am here, because I am *not* here!"

"I am still glad to see you," he said.

I looked at the grave. It would be nice if one of these two Mulvaneys made sense.

"I am glad you are glad," I said coolly.

I had to admit that he had gone to an extraordinary amount of trouble, some of it illegal, to get me here. Jim Mulvaney, the surviving one, anyway, was a good-looking man who had wit, nerve, and the ability to make my underpants wet before he'd even touched me. So why didn't he ever do that when it was convenient?

Now he was trying to do it in the midst of a war zone. In the midst of a war cemetery!

His war, though, not mine. I could have a romance with Jim Mulvaney if that was all I wanted to have in life. Mulvaney was a full day's work. He was his own story. If I hooked up with him, I'd never write any stories of my own.

"Mulvaney," I said, "I'm only staying tonight." This, I realized, was a weakening of my earlier stance. "And I am not sleeping with you."

"I just wanted you to have something to think about."

How could he imagine I didn't?

"A book about me should have more tenderness," my husband says.

I thought he only wanted sex. And why is he changing the subject? I've brought him the manual so he could write his screenplay, not talk about my book.

"You're already getting more than most husbands," I say.

"All you have to do is revise the latest chapter."

Suddenly I understand.

"Mulvaney!" I say. "We are not going to have sex at the cemetery. I am not going to have sex with Jim Mulvaney at Jim Mulvenna's grave."

"If my relatives hadn't come to America, I could have been him."

"Mulvaney, a scene like that at Jim Mulvenna's grave would be a shoo-in for the Worst Sex Writing of the Year contest."

"A lot of famous writers have won that contest."

He needs to be stopped. "I'll tell people that I write bad sex because I have bad sex."

His eyes turn blue like the horizon.

He has, I know, devised a compelling, although not verifiable, counterargument.

"They'll know you made it up."

"And why is that?"

"When sex is really great, you don't remember anything."

I stare back at him. No matter what Jim Mulvaney thinks, he is not the only genius in the universe. "Okay. I admit it. I don't want to write that scene because I can't. I can't remember anything at all about having sex with you. I do not think there is a wife on earth who remembers less."

If you ask me, it is convoluted logic that keeps most marriages alive.

CHAPTER 21

Cold Bed, Cold Heart

Suzie McBreeze's brick house on Owenvarragh Park, off the Andersonstown Road, would have looked at home on Avenue I, even if it was smaller in scale, *attached,* and not across the street from any shul. With its front garden, modest hedges, and climbing ivy, it too had striver's notions.

Mulvaney screeched his T-Bird brakes in the narrow driveway. Suzie's house reminded *him,* he said, of the place in Queens where he lived when he was the Short Paperboy. "We never had British soldiers in Hollis, though."

Mulvaney had his own key. Inside, the McBreeze daughters watched black-and-white television in a minuscule living room; Suzie had stayed on at the Felons Club, hopeful that Mother's Night would really become one.

"Wood?" I asked, sniffing smoke.

"Peat," Mulvaney said.

It had been warmer *outside*.

BBC News blasted through the frigid, blurry air. The girls sat, nearly motionless, on a tattered couch, the one, I guessed, my mother had so valiantly offered to rehabilitate along with several Project Children kids.

Suzie's couch was, indeed, the hobo king of couches, lumpy as oatmeal, covered with patchwork rather than upholstery. Swatches overlapped so that stripes ran into swirls into polka dots, all of them awful and, in keeping with what I could now identify as local tradition, tinged with olive green. Even her daughters, in layers of bulky sweaters, could not camouflage it, beautiful though they were. The youngest sipped from a bottle of orange soda while she plucked out pieces of gray stuffing. The eldest bent over the middle child and gave her a gentle slap on the wrist. "Mummy told you it's dangerous to do that!"

"Yew sound like a fookin' Peeler," the little one said.

The big sister—thirteen, I guessed—held her hand up and was about to slap the little girl again when she turned, saw me, and flipped off the television.

"That yer sweetie, Jimmy Mulvenna?" she asked. Even the kids had known his plan.

I was introduced to the McBreeze girls from eldest to youngest—Aisling, Suzannah, Bridget—a conglomeration of blond hair, curled and straight; strategically placed freckles; and long limbs in need of athletic fields. I couldn't imagine any of them growing up to look like their mother. But how early did the women here start to fall apart? We crowded together in the living room. A photograph of a balding, distant man stood on a small end table, next to the potbelly. A brick of peat simmered slowly through its grated door.

"Suzie's husband," Mulvaney said.

Martin McBreeze, in a crew cut and white button-down short-sleeved shirt, could, indeed, have been at IBM instead of in the IRA, if the immigration process had only touched his family, too. Now, though—hair and shirt notwithstanding—I could only picture him on the run in America, hiding perhaps under Dan Tubridy's sink.

Above Martin hung a photograph of a handsome teenage boy in a school uniform. "Our Kieran's doing his time," Suzannah, the middle child, informed me. "He burned down a bus."

"Mummy says it was because he misses our da," Bridget, the youngest, added as she brushed a waft of couch stuffing from her sweater.

Next to their incarcerated brother, inside a frame made from a miniature carved harp, there was a gleaming new photograph of Suzie—and Mulvaney—with Peter King, the Nassau County Comptroller, a Long Island Republican, who happened to be an *Irish* Republican as well. King, certain he could broker a peace deal, visited Northern Ireland frequently even though any number of Protestant paramilitaries had threatened to kill him.

The girls invited me to sit on the couch. As I did, one of the swatches fell to the floor, exposing more stuffing.

"This couch is a mortification," Aisling said as she squeezed next to me.

"My mother's is worse," I said.

Mulvaney motioned with his eyes to meet him in an alcove that turned out to be the kitchen, tinier than the living room and reeking of cooking fat. It had a sink, a small icebox, a cooker but no oven, and a heavy mahogany cabinet that didn't belong. He moved the cabinet aside to reveal a door.

Behind it was a sliver of a room. The floor was covered, Mulvaney-style, with old newspapers, half-filled cups of tea— no coffee here?—reporter's notebooks, discarded plaid shirts, and a camera that I bet had no film.

We stood, facing one another, in front of a small window. I pulled up the blind. Nothing else you could do without involving the bed, even if it was a single.

"Need a nap?" he asked, moving forward.

I moved back, almost tripping over his doctor's bag.

"Make the bed warm," he said, leaving me there.

Traveling for one day and drinking for two had not been a restful combination. Neither was meeting the IRA, living or dead. Mulvaney returned with two glasses of whiskey. I could barely stand. But I was not going to sit on that bed.

"Is that Powers?" I asked him, taking one and gulping.

"Why?"

"Suzie said that Powers makes men mean."

"You believe that?" He looked prepared to be anything but mean.

"No, I don't believe that," I said.

"What do you believe, then?"

I took another large gulp. "I believe that you are many things, Mulvaney. But not mean."

"What else?"

"Even whiskey couldn't make you mean. But it also couldn't make you any crazier."

"What else?"

"I believe that it is almost summer here and freezing and I want to go to Paris."

"What else?" His blue eyes gleamed like a man who expected the answer he wanted.

I didn't know.

He followed me back into the kitchen.

"Here," he said, handing me my knapsack. I checked and, yes, the wallet and passport were inside. "But I hope," he said, for the second time in less than twenty-four hours, "that you don't go."

I looked around to see if any PR men had been asked to stand guard.

Upstairs, the McBreezes had three small bedrooms, but the girls and their mother slept together in one.

I flopped on a bed in one of the empty rooms and felt nothing until I woke hours later but still before dawn, my fingers and toes numb from the cold, my body shaking in an icy fever. I'd never felt chilled like this, not even in the dead of a New York January. If I was going to copulate out of the faith, I should have picked a man whose ancestors came from a warmer climate. New York was crawling with men with Italian last names. I could have been in Florence.

I slid my knapsack out from under the pillow, put on my carry-on sweater, but felt no warmer.

"Mulvaney," I said, "move over." I put my knapsack down at the side of his bed, lifted off his blanket, and saw he was naked. How did he survive this?

Shivering, I examined his setup.

Mulvaney was plugged in.

And he'd called me a princess?

This had to be the only electric blanket in the house.

He didn't wake, so I pushed him. He moved. I got in and carefully placed my cold feet between his warm legs. He grunted and groaned. In his sleep he tried to put his hand inside my jeans. I pulled it out.

"Mulvaney," I said, "this arrangement is climatic."

Not climactic.

But I dreamed of him. I dreamed he had been arrested for bootlegging all the whiskey in Ireland, North and South. Not a political crime. But it was, as the song goes, a capital offense. The electric chair. Sans blanket.

As they dragged him out of the courtroom, in handcuffs and chains, to meet his Maker, he told the bewigged judge that if it wasn't for me he would not have needed any whiskey at all.

I woke to his hand back in my jeans.

"Is it okay?" he asked.

"Only because you have a death sentence," I said, not sure if I meant it.

Sex for Siding (resumed)

I go downstairs, freeze.

Finally, I walk out into the sunshine.

And across the street.

"So you would like to learn," the contractor says.

"Actually," I say, "I'd be more interested in having someone do it for me."

Now the contractor does turn from his work. The lines around his green eyes crinkle and I remember a professor I once knew.

"For you?" he says.

"Yes, a favor."

He says nothing.

"Do you think that's possible?" I ask.

"I think that's very possible," he says. "But nothing fake."

"I don't fake."

"Not even fake Victorian?"

"I despise fake Victorian."

"I knew you would."

"I also despise real Victorian," I say.

He crinkles again. "I know."

CHAPTER 22

A Nice Irish Doctor

I started, with Mulvaney's help, to take off my clothes.

So I must have meant what I said.

Suddenly, metal crashed against metal.

"We're being bombed," I noted.

Unimpressed, he tossed my jeans on his growing heap of floor detritus. "It's just bin lids. Garbage can tops. The women bang them when the Brits are coming."

The noise was deafening. "They should try reciting Longfellow."

He tossed my underpants on the floor.

"It worked for the Americans," I added.

Approaching sirens drowned out the metal; heavy automotive machinery clanged in harmony.

As he leaned in, a lone female voice resounded through the noise. *"How dare you harass these fine people because of their religion! Brits out of Northern Ireland!"*

I jumped out of bed.

"And don't think you can scare me. I, too, come from a place where . . ."

Across the street, framed in the window, my mother stood in front of an armored car. Two young soldiers trained their rifles on her. Undeterred, she railed on.

"A place where people were killed because of the way they worshipped!"

The black taxi that I guessed had delivered her into the midst of the raid—my mother's impeccable timing now an international phenomenon—sideswiped two army jeeps, ran up the sidewalk, turned, and sped away.

I pulled on my clothes. "Mulvaney," I said as I slammed the door on his den of iniquity and clutter, "this is all your fault!"

Suzie, still in a nightgown and pink curlers, ran out the front, just ahead of me. "Do not shoot my mother!" I cried, bursting outside on her heels.

"Barbara!" my mother said as I grabbed her. "Don't be silly." She shook a perfectly manicured red fingernail. "They can't shoot me. I'm an American."

The two rifles were now aimed at the three of us.

From the neighbors' house, a teenage boy in pajamas was shoved out at gunpoint by two more soldiers. The bin lids had died down but now they started up again in earnest.

"Religious persecution!" my mother shouted. *"Do your mothers know what you are doing?"*

"Ma'am," one of the soldiers said, "I'll have to ask you to move on." He had sparse brown stubble on his face, as if he had to work at growing a beard.

"Sonny," my mother said, "I will do no such thing."

The soldier ordered the three of us into Suzie's house. My mother followed Suzie with her fist raised to the sky, her diamond engagement ring—her own symbol of triumph over adversity—glaring up at the puffy Belfast clouds. It still hadn't poured and the bin lidders hadn't stopped banging. Either there were more Brits coming or these people felt solidarity with my mother, further proof of their misguided passions.

"Troublemaking American gunrunners!" the soldier said.

What was he talking about? The soldiers were the only ones who had any guns.

And where the hell was Mulvaney?

The stubbly soldier ordered his partner, a boy with sweaty freckles, to guard us in the living room while he ran upstairs, his boots pounding on the creaky steps. No sound of Suzie's daughters. Mulvaney, I hoped, was hiding them in his room.

"Can I use yer loo?" The freckled boy was now soaked in his own sweat.

Suzie nodded and pointed toward a small room at the far end of the hallway.

"Good," my mother said. "Let's escape." From upstairs we heard dull thuds on the floor as the soldier took apart Suzie's beds. "At least two soldiers still outside," Suzie warned her. "Could be more by now."

My mother eyed the couch. "Then we might as well redecorate."

"Maybe not now, Ida," Suzie said.

"Why don't we just try this fabric on that cushion?"

Suzie gasped as my mother lifted a sheath of material off the couch, uncovering bare yellowed stuffing. She grabbed at the stuffing, and three black matte pistols, wired together by their trigger guards, came up with it.

"Jesus, Joseph, and Mary!" said my Jewish mother, who'd been in Ireland less than forty-eight hours. The door to the loo creaked open. Outside, it began to pour. My mother stuffed the guns back in the couch. Boots creaked on the steps.

By the time the soldiers returned to the living room, my mother was lying across the couch.

"Up!" the stubbly one ordered her. "We have to search all cushions!"

"Just a minute while I get my old bones to move," she murmured.

"Now!" the soldier repeated. He lurched a baby step closer.

At that my mother began to wheeze, as she had done on the airplane, an act I did not expect would work twice in the same war zone. "She's very sick," I said. "If she moves, she could die. If she dies, it could have global implications."

Someone pounded on the front door. "Answer it!" the soldier ordered.

The man at the door was Mulvaney. But a Mulvaney transformed by pinstripes.

"Nice suit," I said. I couldn't imagine where Mulvaney got such an outfit, or, more curiously, how it stayed pressed if he wore it in the rain.

"Mu—" I said.

He put a hand on my mouth. "Talk softly. It's better for your health." His blue eyes shifted down to the bag he carried. The bag the medical examiners had given him. He stepped inside and turned to the soldiers.

"Doctor," I said, wondering if I could make him a Jewish doctor. My mother would at least die happy. "Let me take your bag." I grabbed it out of his hand, turned it so that the Long Island coroner's shield was on the inside.

Mulvaney saw that. "No need," he said, taking the bag back the way I handed it to him.

"My mother is too sick to move."

He nodded.

She wheezed, coughed, stopped. Then she gazed up at Mulvaney, who said nothing. He apparently had everything except a script.

"You will have to move off this couch, ma'am." The solider rubbed his embryonic beard.

"I cannot move without my doctor's approval," my mother said. She put her open hand over her forehead, sighed long, and faked a faint. Mulvaney stared at the soldier, who flinched. My mother opened one eye to watch.

"I will have to examine her on the couch," Mulvaney said.

"We need to search her."

"She is not able to move."

My mother moaned. "He's the best heart surgeon in New York," she said, forgetting she was supposed to have fainted.

More silence.

"I guess you haven't seen the movie," I said. So this place did make people desperate.

The soldier turned to me. "The one about my mother and her heart transplant," I plunged on. "She has a baboon's heart, although in her case one from a larger beast would have been more compatible."

"I need to search her," he repeated. His freckle-faced buddy cowered in the corner.

Mulvaney moved in front of him. "Could be a general someday. Could be a Member of Parliament."

"Excuse me, mister?" He was beginning to look even younger.

"Excuse me, *Doctor*," Mulvaney insisted. "It would seem that you are career material. Political, even."

The soldier moved closer to my mother.

"Kill an American woman and it's all ruined." Mulvaney blocked him. "They put you in this godforsaken place, put you in charge of men fighting the most ridiculous, under-appreciated war of the late twentieth century. I'm sure a smart young man like you understands that most of your countrymen don't want troops here. But you do this, do it well without killing anyone, because every death in Northern Ireland makes the British government look worse...."

The soldier shifted his leg. Then he shifted his rifle to me. I could hear myself sweating.

"So," Mulvaney continued, "they figure they owe you because you were in Belfast. You get promoted twice for every single promotion every guy who went to the Falklands gets. Before you know it, they want you to run for Parliament.... Be a pity to have some old Jewish broad from Brooklyn ruin all that."

On the couch, my mother shifted ever so slightly and cocked an eye at her physician.

"Mister?" the soldier asked.

"*Doctor.*" Mulvaney was undeterred. "You move her, she dies. One old, sick, Jewish-broad tourist from America dies on you, it's as if you killed a whole neighborhood of Catholics. Doesn't help matters that I need to bring her to my lecture at the university tomorrow."

"The BBC is taping it," I added.

"I'll have to search around her," the soldier said.

I held my breath. Each time he dug his weapon behind a pillow, my mother moaned.

"Careful, Soldier," Mulvaney said. "Wouldn't want to accidentally puncture her lung, would we?"

Finally the boy soldier stopped rifle-butting pillows. "We'll be back," he said as his sidekick followed him out the door.

Nobody spoke until the street was clear.

"Good thing I unloaded most of the couch last night," Suzie said.

" 'Sex for Siding'?" Mulvaney is triumphant.

"You can't write sex to save your life. No one in their right mind thinks aluminum siding is sexy."

If they lived in my yellow house, they might.

"Not only can't *you* write sex," I say, "you can't read it unless it's about you."

"You want my opinion and then you're angry at me if I tell you the truth."

"When did I ever *ask* your opinion? You stand over me while I am writing and *offer* it to me."

"Your sex scene is filled with clichés."

I contemplate throwing china at my husband. I'll show him clichés.

"James Dean is not a literary device!" Mulvaney is ranting. "He is a Banana Republic ad campaign." Next he's going to tell me he can't believe anyone could be so stupid.

"Well, Mulvaney," I say, moments before banging the front door behind me, "I would do the same for you if only I could find the right product."

I walk down the street, hoping to run into my contractor. So, Mulvaney doesn't like "Sex for Siding," which happens to be a true-true story? Fine. He never has to know how it ends.

I am going to *make up* my next non-Mulvaney flirtation. And this time it's going in the main text.

CHAPTER 23

Main Text

Would it be hyperbolic to say that the new man I met in Paris looked like Sean Connery?

He had that gray beard, neatly trimmed, and he smiled with his eyes, which were green, not blue.

He was not short, nor was he a medium-sized man who thought he was short and therefore tortured everyone with Napoleonic tendencies he had no right to exhibit.

No, this man was tall and he knew it.

He could be smart and interesting without requiring the world to blow up around him. He knew revolutionaries but he did not live with them. Nor did the revolutionaries he knew all come from the same ethnic group as he did.

He had at least one friend who wasn't a cop, a criminal, or his father's bartender.

I could tell you the specific details of how I met this man, but I don't want to give Mulvaney the satisfaction. Suffice it to say that he was in Paris visiting a sick friend named Samuel Beckett.

Colm McEligot is from Dublin, which means that unlike Mulvaney, he really is Irish. But unlike Mulvaney's friends in Belfast, he is not a hoodlum. He is a Trinity College political scientist, whose area of expertise just happens to encompass the international connections of any number of revolutionary groups, including, but not limited to, the Nicaraguan Sandinistas.

I was sure Colm McEligot could help me fix my career problems, which was *one* of the reasons I followed him back to Dublin. That he looks like Sean Connery, an Irish Sean Connery, is mere coincidence. Despite what all those high-minded literary souls and expensive writing programs tell you, there is no reason why coincidence can't work as well in fiction as it does in real life, where it happens every day without causing any major intellectual rifts.

If Mulvaney can do better, he should go right ahead. Let him figure out a more believable way for me to dump my mother in Paris and save my career. He should not, however, forget that he was the one who got me into this situation. It was his fault that my mother and I had to flee Northern Ireland before she got arrested for gunrunning.

Or was it gun sitting?

Mulvaney says that he would like to expand Marsha McCain's role in this book.

"She's the new kind of Nationalist," he says. "She's looking for a political solution."

Aren't we all, I think.

"Mulvaney," I say, "I'm thinking about taking her out entirely." True-true: She's getting cut down to skin and bones after I use her for a few laughs. "A surfer babe in Sinn Fein. Who would believe that?"

"Maybe nobody has to believe it. Maybe I made her up!"

If he wants to do that, I tell him, he should write his own book.

CHAPTER 24

Dublin Princess

I n the café of the Kilkenny Design Centre on Baggot Street in Dublin, Professor Colm McEligot appeared behind his American exchange students and, with a flourish, served an overflowing plate of cakes, scones, and muffins. Their applause resounded throughout the café.

After a bow gauged to tease, he took a silver flask from the pocket of his clean denim shirt, taut against his chest, and poured a shot of golden liquid into his white coffee mug. He poured for each student, too, but considerably less.

A young man grabbed a cake. "Aw, c'mon, Professor McEligot! A drop more?" he said, faking a Boston accent. "Don't you want us to make you a legend in Harvard Yard?"

"Already am one there, thank you," Colm McEligot replied, his posh Dublin accent gone, his own version of a fake Bostonian in its place. Within minutes he switched to Gaelic, then Spanish, then back to English and so began his tutorial on "Irish Nationalism, America and the Sandinistas."

He saw me watching, smiled with his green eyes and his mouth, and directed me to a nearby table, as if to say I could listen to him but only if I wanted to.

Already this potential romance was progressing better than the yet-to-be-reconsummated one with Mulvaney. From the window next to my table I could see the stone walls of Trinity College as I drank my own cappuccino, a rare beverage in Dublin but not, I suspected, as rare as up North. The foam swirled in its elegant Danish white mug, and across the floor the design center displayed its other wares: clay teapots, pewter flatware, and piles of sweaters, none of them Aran. I got up and walked over to admire a black intarsia with a bold geometric design.

"And what does a Jewish princess make for dinner?" Colm McEligot asked as I passed. This joke had been around New York for decades but he was, I could tell, being gently wry.

"She could make an old Irishman happy," I replied.

"See?" he turned to his students, his green eyes aglow. "I am a true scholar of international relations."

The tutorial ended hours later in Toner's Pub on Baggot Street. Somehow, it dwindled to two. Colm McEligot asked me if I wanted to meet Chaim Herzog. It was not what I had expected him to say but charming nevertheless. Outside, he hailed a nonsectarian taxi and dropped me off at the Kilronan House, a bed-and-breakfast across from the Hebrew Congregation of Dublin, a shul for Catholic Jews that was also the only shul in Dublin. In the morning an invitation to an Irish state dinner for the President of Israel arrived.

CHAPTER 25

Circumstance

Claire, on deadline, announced that the Men Who Didn't Write *Naked Came the Stranger* had unearthed a sex scandal. "Late bloomers," she said. "They nailed the Huntington Dogcatcher."

For an animal story, this had legs. But how many and what kind?

"Six," she said. "But only two human."

"So hind legs guarantee upfront play?"

Claire did not laugh. "I don't think you understand why you are in Dublin."

She was wrong. I was in Dublin because I wanted *Newsday* to send me to Latin America. "I didn't understand why I was in Belfast," I said.

"*That* was because you and Mulvaney belong together. Or, better put, you don't seem able to escape one another."

"Ah, but we did."

"Not for long. Circumstance is very important in romance. And it's a lot more subtle than coincidence. We don't give it enough credit."

Just ask the Huntington Dogcatcher.

"I think I need someone more stable," I said. "Maybe an academic type."

Claire snorted loudly. "Professors are even bigger nut jobs than faltering foreign editors."

"Safari Suit's been torpedoed?"

"Close."

Leisure Suit, she said, wanted to steal the foreign editor's job and had mounted, speaking of dog stories, a campaign worthy of a presidential candidate, claiming, of course, that he could oversee *Newsday*'s world coverage from Ronkonkoma.

Had he noticed that I hadn't returned from the vacation I didn't tell him I was taking?

Silence.

"Well?"

"Listen"—she sounded uncharacteristically sheepish—"this is not a good time. He just found out that you and your mother almost got arrested for gunrunning. . . ."

"Let me talk to him."

"He just threw a clipboard at the trash can."

In the ballroom of the Office of Foreign Affairs, I leaned against a marble pillar, looked up at the carved ceiling and then down again, searching for Colm McEligot.

A woman in white linen trimmed with lace played the harp,

and underneath a Waterford chandelier the three Jewish members of the Dáil, the Irish Parliament, argued about legalizing birth control. The Jews could have had a voting block; they outnumbered Dáil Protestants. But each one of them belonged to a different party.

Chaim Herzog, a determinedly pleasant man who held a ceremonial rather than elected position, stood in the midst of a bevy of Irish diplomats and freestanding pewter vases filled with blue West Cork hydrangeas. A few Gardai—Irish cops— huddled nearby as the President of Israel helped himself to a flute of champagne and a dollop of smoked salmon that could have been lox. He ate it with a grin. According to the morning's *Irish Times,* the Brits in the North, his birthplace, had tried to serve him prawns, also a local specialty but not a kosher one.

Under the chandelier, the Jewish Dáil sex argument escalated. Ben Briscoe was the best known of the trio. His father had been Lord Mayor of Dublin and a hero of the Irish Revolution, which meant that the old man had blown up buildings. These days, though, that was rarely mentioned. Now when a Briscoe made the news, it was over opposition to what was known in every Irish pub as "the Condom Bill."

The crowd grew larger and pushed me so close to Briscoe I had to introduce myself. He said he was impressed that a Long Island newspaper had sent a reporter to cover Chaim Herzog in Ireland, which it hadn't.

The lights dimmed and a spot flooded on the harpist, then moved. Next to her, transformed from professorial by a tux, stood my favorite Trinity political scientist.

"A traditional ballad," he announced and, in an alto, too high for a man but still strong, he began.

When cocks curved throats for crowing
And cows in slumber eeled
She tiptoed out the half door
And crossed her father's fields

Down the mountain shoulders
The ragged dawn light came
And a cold wind from the westland
Blew out the last star's flame

Her father, the strong farmer,
Had horses, sheep and cows,
One hundred verdant acres
   And slates upon his house

And she stole with the starlight
From where her life began
To roam the roads of Ireland
With a traveling tinker man

His hair was brown and curling,
His eyes were brown as well,
His tongue would charm the hinges
Off the gates of hell

Mulvaney has not spoken to me
for two chapters.

CHAPTER 26

Wandering

Whiskey in hand, bow tie perfectly straight, Colm walked toward me. "You shouldn't be singing about hell to a room full of Jews," I said. "Not to mention tinkers."

In Ireland, tinkers—more courteously called "itinerants"—lived on the sides of roads in trucks or trailers. They sold pots for a living and were said to be fighters and thieves and—even worse—Gypsies, and therefore different. Not a good idea to remind Jews that their hosts, Irish though they might be, were capable of oppressing a downtrodden, misunderstood people.

Colm tried to look down my red brocade dress, which I'd bought at the Laura Ashley shop on Dawson Street. I'd told the salesclerk I needed something sedate, befitting a state dinner. Drapery, I'd suggested.

"Hard to see past the material," Colm agreed as Chaim Herzog appeared.

"Professor McEligot!" Colm bowed, exchanged his empty whiskey glass for a flute of champagne, and handed another one to the President of Israel, who took it and then the professor's arm. "We Jews, like the Irish Itinerant People, are wanderers. I myself, as you know, wandered out of Ireland and became President of the Promised Land."

As Herzog moved on, Colm took a triumphant taste of champagne. A drop hit his beard. Golden and gray. "Let's get out of here," he said, green eyes aglow. "Would you like to see where Leopold Bloom lived?"

I felt the kind of thrill that comes from being terrified. "He lived in Joyce's imagination," I said, trying to buy time to think. Wandering Jews, I guessed, were the evening's theme.

The lines around Colm's eyes formed arrows directing me to the center, the green. "Well?" he asked. "Would you like to see the manifestation of Joyce's imagination?"

Suddenly, I heard stomping.

"Hey, Sarge, how ya doin?"

I turned, hoping that I had eaten a bad piece of smoked salmon or that I was in a bad movie or a bad book based on a bad movie, all of which would have been better than the sight I saw: Mulvaney at the ballroom entrance, shaking hands, vigorously, with one of the Garda following Chaim Herzog.

The Non-*Naked* Men had told me a wanted poster with Mulvaney's picture hung in Foresto Tuxedo in Mineola. It wasn't him they were after, as much as the tuxedo he had forgotten to return in October 1975.

I know where it is, I thought.

The tie was askew, the shirt untucked, the jacket wrinkled and unbuttoned and perched precariously on his shoulders. He took a bottle of champagne from the nearest waiter and popped the cork, which jettisoned off the marble pillar, flew up and hit the wooden carving of the ceiling, sped down, wound its way through the lace of the harpist and the strings of her harp. It knocked over a pewter vase, crashed into a crystal tear of the chandelier, and finally fell to the ground.

Having defied many of the principles of physics, Mulvaney walked toward us. He put one arm around Colm and the other around me, his hand dangling just over the front of my dress.

"Mulvaney!" Colm McEligot said with glee.

"You know each other?" I asked, wishing for a better line.

Mulvaney stared at me in incredulous blue. "You kiddin'? Colm McEligot's famous. You never saw him on *Sixty Minutes*? Every foreign correspondent in the world's quoted him at some time or other."

"We were just leaving," I said, moving Mulvaney's hand aside.

"So soon? The two of you?"

I nodded.

"I thought we had a good time together in Belfast."

"Mulvaney!" I shouted as Colm McEligot looked on with what could best be described as detached academic concern. "There was a couch full of guns in Belfast. It kind of ruined that good time." So, I thought, did the red-haired Marsha McCain.

"I got you close to the action."

"Mulvaney, we're supposed to be reporters! That close is too close."

"Would you like to join us?" Colm, ever the gentleman, asked Mulvaney. "On a stroll through Jewish Dublin?"

"He wouldn't," I said, glaring at Mulvaney, who glared back.

"Not only wouldn't I!" Mulvaney retorted, as hard as any postcard of rocks. "I won't!"

"Cognac?" Colm offered his flask to me outside the Georgian doors of the Foreign Affairs Building, and I took a swig. "It will make you feel better."

"I believe that, even if it is stupid," I said as we stood facing St. Stephen's Green.

"Nothing stupid about a booze prescription. It's as old as civilization itself."

We turned away from the Green and walked deeper into South Dublin, where the streets turned residential and less grand.

"So is it true that the Irish are the lost tribe of Israel?" I asked.

Colm put his hand on my shoulder.

"Or are the Jews the lost tribe of Ireland?" he asked.

I left his hand where it was.

"We've had at least a handful here since 1079 and more than a few escaped Portugal in 1496, never worrying about *British* tyranny, of course. Shows a certain lack of forethought, don't you think?"

"Not when faced with an Inquisition."

"How could you forget Cromwell?" Colm asked.

I hadn't. I wondered if I ever would.

We passed rows of squat, attached brick houses, smaller even than the ones in Belfast. A decent American contractor could do wonders with them. Then we turned onto Clanbrassil Street, a wider, equally crumpled commercial block, and stopped at a row of swankier Georgian houses. Colm opened the iron gate leading to one of them.

"I thought Leopold Bloom lived on Eccles Street?"

"Only tourists go there! This is before."

There was a green door. Number 52. A rosebush wound its way up near a plaque, that read "Here, in Joyce's imagination, was born Leopold Bloom, citizen, husband, father, worker, the reincarnation of Ulysses."

Joyce's imagination. My very words. Maybe, I thought, I could get a job writing literary plaques in Dublin.

"Jews don't believe in reincarnation," I said.

Colm nodded, parked himself on the front stoop, put the now-empty flask of cognac back into his breast pocket, and picked a rose. He put the rose in his mouth and did a brief flamenco step, without touching a thorn.

"We could break in," I said.

Surprised, he looked at me. What was it with Irish men? They try to seduce you, then look aghast if you merely give them a hint they might succeed.

Colm dug back into his tuxedo pocket, fished around, and came up with a corkscrew so thick and substantial it could have been made from antique Dublin silver.

"Are you going to screw the house open?" I asked. "Or open the house to screw?"

He threw it hard, like a young man. The first-floor window shattered. Then he carefully slid his hand through the broken glass, unlatched a lock, and opened the window.

"Care for a climb?" he asked.

But it was a question. Not an answer.

Still, he asked it.

It was what I'd wanted, wasn't it? A suitor with some mischief that wasn't lethal. Vandalism over Felony Murder. So why wasn't I sure?

"You're not the woman I thought you were," he said after a long pause.

"You think I'm Molly Bloom," I said, hoping I could stop there. With only a B.A. in English, it would be reckless to use any more Joycean allusions to delay sleeping with this man while I made up my mind.

"Molly Bloom," I boomed out over Clanbrassil Street, throwing caution to the wind. "Molly Bloom would have been climbing out the window."

"That, dear, would have been Eccles Street," he said.

I had to think fast. Did I want to sleep with Colm McEligot? Or would anyone who wasn't Mulvaney do the trick?

"Could you become a serial offender?" I asked.

Mulvaney says that I am incapable

of writing more than four very short, dull chapters without him as protagonist. He says that even when I am not writing about him I am reflecting his essence and that I do that even while showing something he is not.

"Essence?" I say.

I tell him that a man who wants a woman has to find ways to keep her.

CHAPTER 27

Gypsy Music

I called Claire to ask her if Leisure Suit had forgiven me for the guns yet. Or the vacation.

"How the hell should I know?" Claire exploded transatlantically. "He won't even lean across the desk to talk to me! He just sends messages! While you were gone, they put Message Pending on all the computers and he blinks it on and off a million times a day, like the crazy person he is. My whole life is Message Pending! Message Pending, *Message PENDING, MESSAGE PENDING!!!*"

Sounded familiar.

I reminded Claire that it was her fault, too, I was here.

"You ought to thank me," she snapped. "Losing a job at *Newsday* is the best thing that could happen to a person."

So I *was* getting fired.

"And I'm helping you to find true love."

I hung up on her.

"Look," she said when she called back, "I'm sorry. Give me some time. Things are worse here than you can imagine. On top of everything else, there's going to be a *Naked Came the Stranger* sequel."

"*Naked Returned the Stranger?*"

"Worse. The Men Who Wrote *Naked Came the Stranger* are teaming up with the Men Who Didn't. Even worse, they are going to write it *on Message Pending!*"

"Electronic *and* epistolary?"

"Only the Men Who Didn't still can't. The dogcatcher story bombed. We had to print numerous corrections."

It made for a wonderful collaboration, though.

Young men who couldn't write sex.

And old men who didn't use computers.

How nice, I thought, when I heard a knock the next morning. The Kilronan House has sent me breakfast in bed. Maybe I don't need a job.

I stepped out of the bathtub, tied a large towel around myself, and opened the heavy pine door. But instead of room service with eggs and blood pudding, I found Mulvaney wearing an awful green sport jacket.

"Get dressed," he said as he merrily pushed his way in, handing me a newspaper and a sausage roll and eyeing my towel as if he hoped it would fall off. His black doctor's bag thumped onto the floor. "I have a great story to show you."

"Mulvaney, you look like a game show host." I returned the pastry.

"It's a big international story—with a Huntington angle."

I shook my head.

"If you don't write it, I will."

I considered the impact, on me, of a *Newsday* Sandinista story with local implications—and Mulvaney's byline.

"I'll give you an hour," I said. "For old times' sake."

Outside, he sped along, ten large steps ahead of me. I shouted from behind, through a sea of pedestrians. "You remember insisting I come with you?" He slowed and I tried to enjoy this brief moment of moderation. We had walked beyond St. Stephen's Green, past the Foreign Affairs mansion, before Mulvaney, his green jacket flapping in the breeze, spoke again.

"Look for Clanbrassil," he said.

I stopped and shivered in the weak Irish sun. "*You* are taking me to the house where Leopold Bloom was born?"

"Nah. But the book's not bad. Needs more plot—and a better protagonist. That one's an empty suit. Guy takes your wife, ya shoot him. At the least."

You could accuse Mulvaney of many things, but being a Joycean wasn't among them. I shivered again. "Do you think anyone would ever let *you* have a gun, Mulvaney?"

"Nope," he said, stopping at a run-down butcher shop. In the window, chickens hung from their necks.

"Look!" he ordered, pointing to a small sign.

It was in Hebrew.

Jim Mulvaney, who had once accused me of being unable to

find a church in Brooklyn when he meant a Jew in the Bronx, had just found a kosher butcher in Dublin. This, I had to admit, wasn't bad. But what was the Huntington angle? An international meat scandal would be great, I thought, then scolded myself. I did not want to visualize a story I didn't have. Classic reporter error.

Mulvaney's chest puffed as he opened the glass front door and gently steered me inside. A petite woman with brown hair as stringy as stew meat smiled from behind the counter.

"And that's her. She's a broad! A broad butcher! A kosher broad butcher. How many of those you seen, *anywhere?*"

His eyes shone blue and white like the Israeli flag.

The butcher wiped her hands on a bloody apron, picked up a chicken, arranged it on a board, and chopped its head off. The cartilage made a loud crack. She did it again—and again—until she had decapitated six chickens. "Bloody rabbi!" she said, smiling at us.

A murder story?

"The Chief Rabbi of Ireland is . . ." Mulvaney said, pausing for drama. "A . . ." He smiled blue. ". . . *vegetarian!*"

I looked at him as if he was nuts.

"He's ruining her business," Mulvaney explained, with his best "I am a sane man" look.

The butcher's thick white fingers tensed. She grabbed more chickens and went at them like an axe murderer presented with a bevy of starlets. "He couldn't leave soon enough for me." Crack! "If he were a real rabbi, he'd be in America." Crack. "America! A place that became great because the people there eat meat!" Crack, crack, crack.

"Mulvaney," I said, not hopeful. "What's the Huntington angle?"

"Easy. Remember that story you wrote, about the Huntington Lawyer's Club?"

How could I forget? I hadn't written one for *Newsday* since. Had he been reading all my pieces, in Belfast?

"Well, this is a story that shows how much more advanced Ireland is than Huntington. There, they don't believe in broad lawyers. Here, they even believe in broad butchers!"

So this was Mulvaney's plan? I'd save my job by writing about a kosher girl butcher while he covered the Irish Republican Army?

"I'm leaving," I said.

"It's a great story," he said. "And there's another one in Belfast about a man who rides a horse-drawn carousel into Catholic and Protestant neighborhoods. Nobody else can go back and forth like that without getting shot."

I remembered dreaming of Mulvaney's death sentence. Now I imagined him begging for his life and insulting the executioner.

Outside, ahead of us on St. Stephen's Green, a tinker woman, her face smudged with fake dirt, sat on the sidewalk. She held a baby in one arm and extended a crumbling Styrofoam cup with the other. "Coppers?" she asked. "Have any coppers?"

Mulvaney handed her a five-punt note.

"Since when did you become a social worker?"

He scowled blue. "I'll have you know that Mulvaney is a tinker name."

Of course. The wild eyes, the flashes of temper. The inability to walk slowly or stay in one place.

The deranged ideas that he believed made sense.

Mulvaney could easily be descended from a long line of Irish Gypsies who lived on whichever side of the road of whichever town suited them at the moment.

"How do you know it's a tinker name?" This would be important if we ever had children. We wouldn't, though.

"The PR man at the Irish consulate in New York," he said.

"Hell of a way to get the press on your side."

"I just want you on my side," he said.

Why did Mulvaney do this to me every time I wanted to flee?

"You should have thought of that before you left me for Ireland, moved in with the IRA, got my mother closer to violence than she's been since 1919, and then tried to win me back with two of the stupidest feature stories on the face of the earth."

"Okay, I'll give you Armagh Prison."

"You're giving me a correctional facility?"

"Filled with IRA broads, and the Brits are torturing them. They're making them take off their clothes ten, twelve times a day."

"The male guards?" I said.

"No. It's broads torturing broads."

It *had* sounded too good to be true. "They're in prison, Mulvaney. They're bomb throwers and gunrunners. Why shouldn't they be searched?"

"You don't get it. Irish broads hate to take off their clothes."

"Not for you, apparently."

On a wrinkled single sheet of reporter's notebook paper, he wrote down what he claimed was the name of a prisoner. "She's my cousin," he said as he handed it to me. "I swear."

"Long Island angle," I muttered, crumpling the paper into the pocket of my skirt. "Mulvaney, why don't you just suggest I do some mildly offbeat, overdone travel story? I can see it now: " 'Paris in Winter, Spain Before the Tourists...' "

"Pamplona without bulls," he said. "Not a bad idea."

• •

I agreed to have coffee with him, only because it was already noon and I needed a jolt of something. My uneaten sausage roll stuck out from the pocket of his green jacket, symbolizing nothing as much as our rotting romance. "Anyplace but the Kilkenny Design Centre," I said.

"What's that?" he asked.

I'd gulp my coffee—the only way to drink most coffee in Dublin—say goodbye to Mulvaney forever, and meet Colm McEligot for lunch. I'd get enough insider Sandinista poop to let me pass Leisure Suit and go directly to Safari. I'd save that guy's job, he'd be eternally grateful, and I'd never have to go to Ronkonkoma again.

"Leisure Suit's not so bad," Mulvaney said. "And he's my boss again. I'm his only foreign correspondent."

Safari Suit, fighting for his job, had apparently considered it prudent to decline to supervise Mulvaney abroad.

I followed him into another ratty storefront, where he pulled out a metal chair for me.

The tablecloths were paper, as were the plates. A waiter—husky with long brown hair pulled back in a ponytail—set our table with plastic forks and knives, Dixie cups, and menus handwritten on paper torn from school notebooks.

I took a quick look, curious to see what the worst sandwich shop in Dublin might serve.

Lunch
Prix fixe——Seven Pounds
Escargot
Cream of Carrot Soup
Mixed Greens

Lemon Ice
Pigeon with Currants
Assorted home-baked tarts, coffee, tea
French cheese plate

"Wait here," Mulvaney said.

"Mulvaney!" I said. "What is this place?" But as I spoke he charged out the door, returning less than five minutes later, brandishing a bottle of Château Margaux. "No liquor license, I forgot."

"Mulvaney, I said coffee."

The ponytailed waiter appeared with a corkscrew. "Shay Beano," he said, introducing himself. "Welcome to Chez Beano. The only seven-course, seven-punt French meal in Ireland."

"The IRA loves this place," Mulvaney said.

"I'm leaving," I said, for the second time that morning. Mulvaney took my arm and poured me a cup.

Men who pour well, even if they are pouring into Dixie cups, look you in the eye to determine whether this is something you'd like to drink. As the wine hit the wax bottom of the cup, it occurred to me, yet again, that I had never seen a man pour better than Mulvaney.

But why did anyone think you could base a relationship on that?

Mulvaney presents me with an outline

for the rest of the book. Now he wants to write the book he wants me to write about him.

You could measure the temerity of this on a Richter scale.

At the bottom of his outline he adds a handwritten note:

"Re: Colm McEligot. NO CONSUMMATION."

"Mulvaney," I say, "not only might there be consummation, Colm McEligot might be the protagonist."

"Har-de-har-har," he says.

"Mulvaney," I say, tears filling my eyes, "you watched *The Honeymooners.*" I have to fight not to let this turn my head.

"Just recently," he admits. "I did it for you."

No, I say to myself. No. No. No.

I harden. "It's too little too late. I don't know where I'm going with you in this book. With Colm, I know. He's going to give me a great story about the Sandinistas, and *Newsday* will send me to Latin America. . . ."

"You can't take *me* out of *The Jim Mulvaney Story,*" Mulvaney says.

"Mulvaney," I say, "this has been a misdirected project from day one, from the day we decided that I would write your life story. You, Jim Mulvaney, were never meant to be in a memoir, even one written by your wife. Particularly one written by your wife."

"I was the last white guy—"

"Mulvaney, would you listen to me! Every time I tried to write the truth about you, you changed the story on me. Anyone who is so disturbed by the bare, unadorned truth as you are just cannot be in a memoir. You pushed me into this."

"You're blaming me because you're having an affair!"

"It's a novel, Mulvaney."

"It's a novel now? Good. Then just have Colm McEligot murdered. This book is filled with potential suspects. It would be a waste not to use them."

"Mulvaney, it just clicked with him and me."

"You need to make yourself hotter for *me*," he says. "As for the tenderness, I may die from the chill, waiting."

"Why is this always my responsibility? Why can't you be hotter? You could be a little more charming, too."

"If you write me any more charming, people won't believe it's true."

"It isn't. So don't assume you can tell me what to do with Colm McEligot."

"You think putting some old Irish guy in it is going to make it sexier?" Mulvaney asks.

"Colm McEligot," I say, "is the rare old Irish guy who actually is sexy."

The Real Mulvaney is visiting and has borrowed my computer to check his e-mail. But now he stops, grabs his cane, and stands, poised to defend the attractiveness of old Irish men. Real ones. Supposedly. He is a bit hobbled by age, but not enough so that he stays off Internet sites for lovelorn senior citizens. He growls, sits back down, and mails out a touched-up photograph of himself.

• •

"Mulvaney," I say, "at this point my character is about to lose her job because of things that your character did. If you want to stay in this book, heretofore known as *my novel,* you need to give me a compelling narrative reason to keep you."

CHAPTER 28

Hansel and Gretel

The next morning I boarded a plane to Bilbao, delighted to be running after my own story. Pity the poor girl stuck with an interreligious carousel, or a bevy of overmodest revolutionaries.

Or a Kosher Irish Butcheress.

Like many Latin American tales, Colm McEligot's began in Spain.

At the Design Centre we'd talked over cappuccinos late into the afternoon, perusing centuries-old Iberian politics until he finally told me I was beautiful and wrote down the alias of a Basque assassin who wanted to talk.

"This will make the Nicaraguans comprehensible," he'd promised.

Now, seated on the plane, I closed my eyes to ponder the career opportunities an exclusive interview might provide.

The overhead compartment opened with a jolt and someone dumped a heavy bag inside.

"Doctor," greeted the flight attendant.

I opened one eye, hoping against hope for a Castilian cardiologist and, instead, saw a glimmer of pinstripes, now wrinkled. "Goddamnit, Mulvaney! What are you doing here?"

"I'm looking for a fugitive who killed some Spanish honcho. Years ago. But he ain't ever talked."

It took me a moment. Then I understood.

Colm McEligot had tipped us both off to the same story. It was, I had to admit, a plot development hard to resist.

Which didn't mean I wouldn't try.

"I know where to find the guy," Mulvaney said, his eyes grinning blue as a poker chip.

I still didn't.

"But I don't know the name he uses."

Being handed different parts of the same story, by the same questionable source/character, was bad enough. Worse was that we'd pitched this story to different—and viciously competing—editors at *Newsday*.

As I had guessed he would, Safari Suit had agreed to send me on this story I proposed, as a last-ditch attempt to keep his job. Mulvaney must have heard—my Spanish assignment would have lasted about five seconds as a secret in Ronkonkoma—and leaned on his renewed friendship with Leisure Suit.

And on Leisure Suit's craven, if provincial, desire to be Foreign Editor himself.

Mulvaney pulled a mangled handful of Irish punts from the pocket of that ratty suit. Where were his other sartorial attempts at satire? The stained plaid shirts, the never-to-be-returned tuxedo, the green sport jacket? Finally, he excavated a small notebook and, as we took off, ordered Rioja for two, which, on this particular morning, seemed like a good idea.

He poured. I tried not to look.

"Are we working together?" he asked, handing me my cup.

"Nope."

"How ya gonna find the guy?"

"Herri Batasuna," I said. The ETA-backed party, the Spanish moral equivalent of Sinn Fein. "They must have a PR man."

"Look," he said, blue eyes wet with red wine, "don't believe me if you don't want to, but that Herri Batasuna PR man won't give up a thing. The guy doesn't talk. He makes your buddy at Huntington Hospital sound like the biggest canary ever to leave a dropping on the L.I.E."

"He can't be that bad."

"Oh yeah? How about not bragging about past escapades. Not even if you confessed and did time. How can you run a subversive organization without a little boasting?"

"So I'll find him myself."

"And how will you get it in the paper?"

"Safari Suit."

"*He* just capitulated to Leisure. This morning."

•   •

I sat back and gave the overhead a dirty look.

Mulvaney poured me another airline cup full of Rioja. "This romance—"

"It is not a romance, Mulvaney."

"It has too much staking of turf. Why can't we just work together?"

"Because you will do something underhanded."

"I promise to share all bylines."

I didn't believe him. But I had a nebulous interview subject and now, without Safari Suit, a shakier chance of publication. I knew defeat when I saw it.

"Deal," I said as I unenthusiastically clinked plastic against plastic. "So where is this guy?"

"We'll have to drive there. I know the name of the bar. But I need his current alias."

"What for?"

"Code. The only way he'll talk."

"Xanti Zarate," I said.

Mulvaney's eyes widened. I had never seen a poker chip *that* blue.

"Mulvaney," I said, "do not for a moment think this means I am sleeping with you."

At the airport we rented a SEAT, a tiny Spanish automobile. "Flimsy car," Mulvaney said, as if he was a man who typically drove a Cadillac.

There was a silence during which I wondered how the King of Duct Tape was going to make idle conversation on a long drive with an old girlfriend who hated his guts but needed him at the moment.

"All that time we spent together and you never told me why you killed your kindergarten teacher."

"You never asked."

"I think I did."

"You wouldn't get it. It's too Freudian."

"Why wouldn't I get Freud?"

I sighed. "Okay, on the first day of school—September, warm—my mother dressed me in wool pants and a sweater."

He grimaced, the way men do when they want to signal that fashion does not interest them. Interesting, coming from him, the prince of strange getups.

"That kindergarten teacher ruined my first day of school. She was an old biddy who dyed her hair red. She put on too much rouge and it got stuck in her wrinkles. And she had favorites—little girls in crinolines named Valerie. She took one look at my pants, glared at my mother, and said, 'Mrs. Fischkin, would you please send your daughter to school tomorrow dressed like a girl.' "

"So?"

"Forget it, Mulvaney."

"How'd your mother take it?"

"She paid no attention. The other class had this nice lady with a long gray ponytail and her name was Miss Sunshine."

"That's Mulvaney-true," Mulvaney said.

"Go look up the records. The other teacher was Miss Sunshine."

"Then she made it up."

"Mulvaney," I said, "you, a person who makes up everything, are suddenly taking offense? Inconsistency! That's your other big problem! So what if 'Miss Sunshine' was a made-up name? For a kindergarten teacher it was a very nice name. It showed that she cared about her students, even in the unlikely instance that she was hiding from the feds or in some sort of elementary school–based witness protection program. If *my* teacher had a different name, she might have lived longer."

"So you killed your kindergarten teacher because you didn't like *her* name?"

"No, she developed facial spasms in the middle of reading 'Hansel and Gretel.' "

"You poisoned her?" His blue eyes turned cold, murderous, delighted. "Did you cry?"

"Nope. I just sat there and counted my blessings. Her last words were 'Valerie, get the principal.' "

"What'd you tell your mother?"

"The true-truth. 'Hey, Mom, my teacher's dead.' "

He took one hand off the steering wheel, put it on mine. I thought that was strange until I reminded myself, yet again, that Mulvaney and I met covering a murder.

"Did you smile?" he asked.

"Let's just say I had the demeanor of a restrained yet satisfied victor."

Mulvaney thinks he can set up the conclusion of this book so that it looks like, at every twist and turn, I need him.

"Mulvaney," I say, "it's a nice development. But it's not enough to make a woman hand over her novel."

"You're kidding. It's a brilliant interplay of characters. This is how you start to tie an ending together."

Screwball comedy may have its limitations.

But simple endings are not among them.

You can always turn another twist.

CHAPTER 29

Mysteries of Spain

Pamplona was, indeed, without bulls.

Mulvaney stopped in front of the only taverna not shuttered and peered through its open window. "No one's drinking," he said.

From inside came a long high scream—a little girl, terrified. Angry, too.

In the distance, police sirens roared closer. Two cars skidded to a halt and four oversized officers barreled out of them. Their stomachs hung over their pants. Together, they had six hairy facial moles, three guns in waist holsters, and a nightstick.

No time with Mulvaney was ever quiet time. Who needed bulls?

Two of the cops leaned against their car. The other two swung open the taverna doors. We followed them toward the escalating screams, through the barroom with its rough-hewn wooden walls dotted with alternating portraits of dozing shepherds and ferocious lumberjacks. They led us past a carved sign—*"Damas"*—and into the dark heart of those screams, the ladies' toilet.

A crowd of *damas*—some *hombres,* too—stood around a thin man, an El Greco type, as he swung an axe at the heavy wrought-iron hinges of a wooden stall door, thick like the walls.

"Xanti Zarate," Mulvaney said, out loud and triumphant again.

"Are you sure?" I wasn't. Too easy.

"Be with you in a minute," the axeman replied.

No way would I show Mulvaney that this impressed me.

At each whack the little girl behind the door screamed. A brown and white mutt yapped happily at my feet.

I hoped this wasn't going to be another dog story. But you never could tell.

The spectators chattered, their words ancient, heavy, and decidedly not Spanish. "What are they saying?" Mulvaney asked.

Basque was not among the foreign languages offered by Midwood High School.

A cop blew a whistle.

The man put down his axe. "Ah," he said, sweating over his black leather jacket. Then, in respectful bourgeoisie Spanish, he told the officers that his small daughter, claustrophobic un-der the best of circumstances, had accidentally locked herself in the toilet and was now entombed by the heavy door. There wasn't even enough space to crawl out.

The cop called outside on his radio, the crowd chattered in that hard, old tongue, and then, finally, noticing Mulvaney and me, went silent.

The two extra officers appeared with two ladders. Xanti Zarate, Basque assassin, put one against the stall and lowered the other gently inside and then softly cooed the solid words of his dying language to his daughter, who did not stop screaming even as she climbed and was scooped into her fa-ther's arms.

Once on the ground, though, she grinned and plumped her wheat-colored pigtails. Around her neck she wore a large gold locket.

I bent down and the dog yapped again at my feet, as if it knew me. But if it did, it would also know how I felt about pets.

"Bonita!" I said to the girl, pointing to her locket. She was about five and opened it to show me a photograph of a dark, slight woman. "I speak English," she announced. "And Euskera. I am not supposed to speak Spanish. Do you speak Euskera?"

"Oh my God!" I said, staring hard at the picture. I knew I'd never forget those eyebrows.

Mulvaney nodded at me.

Amalia Sanchez, the alleged Nicaraguan last seen in the Huntington Hospital emergency room, had been Basque all along.

Talk about a Long Island angle.

"I'm not allowed to tell you where my mother is now," the little girl said. The dog yapped at me again.

"Danielito Ortega Saavedra Perrito!" I said. At the mention of *its* alias, it yapped louder. "You're supposed to be in Managua!"

For years I have wondered what it was that made me agree to drive back to San Sebastian with Mulvaney later that day. We could have rented two rooms in a highway motel outside Pamplona, written, and gone our separate ways. A good business arrangement.

So why did I say yes when he suggested we write on the beach? "Long Island in Spain," he'd said. "Remember how beautiful it looked on the way here?"

Was my head so easily turned by a man who could come up with a good story, even when it had been my own story to start? Was this my lifelong role? To be a link in a giant game of telephone, to start a tale and then have Mulvaney end it in a way I would not expect?

Or was it timing?

We got into the SEAT.

He told me that the Irish had been involved.

"Aren't we always?" he asked.

Self-deprecating humor. Charming.

"I've been checking for a while. I did it for you."

Devotion.

"But without you I wouldn't have known to look. I wouldn't have known there was a story."

Flattery.

Then he took one hand off the steering wheel and poured

Rioja with the other as if his life depended on my reaction to that sip.

Boom.

Crash.

But we didn't, really.

"You helped me turn it into a story," I agreed, taking another sip. He'd probably also helped Colm McEligot to "tip" me off to Xanti.

As the wine hit, though, I remembered San Sebastián, the spectacular view down. Long Island, except better. Long Island with altitude.

I lifted the Rioja and poured him a cup. "I'll tell you what, Mulvaney. We can share the byline."

"Are you sure?" he asked. "I was going to give it all to you."

"I'm sure," I said. And I was. After this I'd have plenty of stories without Mulvaney.

We glowed, together, as we contemplated how this would get good play. The best. Then we reminisced about our reporting.

After the bathroom rescue, departure of the police, and formal introductions, we had all moved to the bar. Xanti ordered a round and assured us that, even as a wanted man wielding an axe, he had not been troubled by the cops in the bathroom. "Law enforcement intelligence is not what it used to be," he'd said, giving his daughter's pigtails a playful tug. "Not anywhere. On Long Island they assumed if I spoke Spanish and sold Communist books, I had to be a Sandinista."

I asked him about Amalia but he shook his head sadly,

called her "my gorgeous victim of history," and regaled us with centuries' worth of Basque struggles against the tyranny of Spain. "We are not Spanish," he said. "We never have been. They conquered us. We only wanted to govern ourselves, speak our own language."

I asked him if the Basques were the lost tribe of Israel, lost again from Ireland.

Xanti, though, was too busy to answer, recounting, as he was, the tale of some old oak tree in Guernica where centuries ago, in what sounded to me like Fairytaleland, Spanish kings had sworn to respect Basque law.

Then the modern Guernica. 1937. A pogrom, Franco-style. Three days of murderous bombing.

"Retribution," he'd said, in an attempt to explain ETA. I didn't buy it but I wrote it down. It was, I knew, leading to the reason why we'd come.

In 1973, Xanti had been one of the ETA thugs who murdered Luis Carrero Blanco, the premier of Spain and, as a Franco crony, no angel himself. Xanti told us this and drank an entire glass of wine, quickly. "We pretended to be a jazz band," he said. The "musicians" rented storage space on a busy Madrid thoroughfare. Inside one of their drums they hid a jackhammer.

By night they dug a tunnel, an elongated bombing post from which they killed the premier in an instantaneous smash-up of shattered metal and glass.

No one, Xanti claimed, had ever told this story, this way, before.

"Why now?" I asked Mulvaney as we approached the glittering Spanish beach city. "And why'd he tell *us*?"

"You already know," he said. "Why does anyone ever tell anything to a reporter? Because they want it out in the open for their own purposes. Herri Batasuna needs to remind the Spanish government that if it doesn't give in to a few political demands, there are competent, experienced bombers waiting in the wings."

"That's sick."

"You expect these people to be posters for Mental Health Week?"

Mulvaney pulled a smaller paper bag out of the one that held the now-empty wine bottle. "Look inside."

I pulled out a gold ring. It had the same design as the charm on Suzie's bracelet. A Claddagh ring. Heart, hands, crown. Love, friendship, loyalty.

Colm had told me the Claddagh came from the Spanish Armada. They'd decorated their shields with it, then sent it back, embossed with jewels, to the Irish women they had conquered, in lieu of conquering the country.

Being an Irish legend, this had the tiniest chance of being suspect.

"Mulvaney, what is this?" In Ireland, the Claddagh was also used on wedding rings.

"You don't have to wear it," he said. "But could you find a better place for it than a paper bag?"

Mulvaney says this chapter is perfect.

He lists what it has: "weapons, drinks, murder, mayhem, jewelry, and love." How, he asks, could you go wrong?

I, though, have another problem, a monumental one.

"Mulvaney," I say, "what I've written is a screwball comedy that romps lightly, much *too* lightly, through international minefields. I'm making light here of some serious end-the-world behavior. Our characters do a Marx Brothers shtick with your doctor's bag while people in Belfast are being shot right and left. Then we glorify the people who give them the guns, who store those guns in their couches. . . . And, to add insult to injury, I am not portraying any of these people as bad. In fact, some of them have a certain charm. . . ."

Mulvaney starts toward my computer, to edit. I pull the chair away before he sits. He stares incomprehensible blue. "What's the big deal?" he asks. "Just explain their motivation."

"Motivation!" I say. "They want to blow up the world!"

"The IRA and the Basques just want their own countries back."

"Yeah, but they'd blow up the rest of the world if they thought that would work. . . ."

"You still could write seriously about the strip searches."

"Mulvaney! Are you even listening? The Brits were strip-searching people who hid guns in their couches. And here we are telling the tales of how we made friends with more people like that?"

"We were not making friends," he says. "We were getting stories."

CHAPTER 30

Love, Friendship, Loyalty

From San Sebastián we called Claire, ready to write.

Claire said she needed Mulvaney and me to dictate budget notes for two stories for the next editorial meeting. "He makes us meet six times a day now," she moaned.

"Just make sure Leisure Suit sees my bylines," I told her.

Main: *Notorious Basque assassin—alleged crimes include killing Spanish premier—hid out in* **Huntington** *for years, disguised as a Nicaraguan alternative bookstore owner and aided by the Irish Republican Army. Xanti Zarate (an alias) fled Long Island last year as his book-*

store——**Liberate Me**——burned, perhaps not by accident, and as he was pursued by Suffolk County detectives for the wrong murder from the wrong venue.

Exclusive, in-depth interview with fugitive Zarate from an undisclosed location in Spain. A wife and alleged accomplice, who lived with Zarate in **Huntington,** is no-show for interview. Will include react from **Suffolk County** Police Public Information Officer, to be provided by bureau in **Ronkonkoma.**

Art: Photo of Daniel Ortega Saavedra (also an alias). Ortega Saavedra is Zarate's dog and a former **Huntington** resident. **By Barbara Fischkin and Jim Mulvaney**

Sidebar: Somewhere in Spain, fugitive Xanti Zarate risks discovery to take his young daughter out to lunch and speak to **Newsday** reporters. When the child accidentally locks herself in a bathroom stall, local police rush to the scene to free her but do not realize they should arrest the father. A European "slice of life," a bright with serious undertones that asks the question "Why isn't law enforcement intelligence——local and international——what it used to be?" Will include additional quote from **Suffolk County** Police Information Officer. **By Jim Mulvaney and Barbara Fischkin**

From his doctor's bag, Mulvaney pulled out two of the thinnest electric typewriters I had ever seen and handed one to me.

"A present," he said. Then he pulled out the phone cord and plugged it into the typewriter.

That Mulvaney could do this amazed me.

We exchanged notes and then, for perhaps the fiftieth time in our ill-fated romance, assessed our different skills.

He wrote fast. I wrote with more flair. He'd write the main. I'd do the sidebar. Then we'd edit each other's stories.

I wrote a lead. It was full of flair. I stopped to watch him. I had always liked to watch him write. He wrote in a fury as if nothing else, and everything else, in the world mattered. With the right facts, his hands could explode in a flat second.

He watched me watching him.

"It's very hot in this room," I said.

Mulvaney opened a window. A warm breeze arrived from the ocean. It cooled my forehead but inside I felt like a brick of peat, one that could warm all of Ireland.

But we were in Spain.

"You are right," he said, and slowly unbuttoned the white shirt he wore with his suit pants. The jacket had disappeared miles ago. As he undid the buttons, he looked at me.

I wrote another paragraph. Mulvaney stripped to his underwear. Nervously, I flipped through my notes, trying to find a good quote. When I couldn't find one, I took off my skirt.

Mulvaney picked up his typewriter and pulled out the plug. "It has batteries, too," he explained.

Then he plumped the pillows on the bed and set up an office there. "Try writing here," he said. "The sheets are cooler."

I looked. They were white satin with ripples like small mounds of snow.

I moved.

Suddenly I had no more need for quotes.

"These are great stories," I said, although we were not writing at all. Instead, slowly, we discovered how it felt to speak freely in your own ancient language, to live in a country that had the right name, its correct old name.

Later, Claire agreed the stories *were* great. "I've never known either of you to write as well," she said.

We went out and hit one tapas bar after another. Off the main square, the Parte Vieja, a man sang in Euskera. "He made up his own songs," Mulvaney assured me.

Well, if anyone would know . . .

Around his neck, he wore the camera he had used to take a picture of Xanti's dog, the only photograph we'd been permitted. We almost didn't get that one, because Mulvaney had no film. Then he found a roll in his doctor's bag.

I started to take Mulvaney's picture and he showed me how to focus. That when he tried, he could focus, intrigued me. He took me by the shoulders and we danced, accompanied by our own Basque soloist.

"You dance worse than your father," he said.

"No, Mulvaney, you dance worse than my father. I dance worse than you."

"Why do you always have to be so competitive?"

"Being the best is best," I said. "Otherwise you should be the worst. The middle is boring."

Dancing with Mulvaney felt more like another activity. I didn't tell him because I finally understood that he did not get metaphors. I had tried for months to decipher what it meant when he walked too fast. He used to say that it was obvious. He walked too fast because the rest of the world moved too slow.

We did not return to the hotel until dawn. "Mulvaney," I said, "now you are walking too slow."

"The ring?" he asked.

"I have it," I said. "It's in my pocket. I need to think."

"You're not going to throw it away, are you?"

"Why would I do that?"

He looked relieved. I had spent so much time thinking about myself as Jewish that I had neglected to properly identify Mulvaney as Catholic.

"Remind me again why we didn't turn in Xanti Zarate?" I ask Mulvaney. "As you remember, there was no dearth of cops."

"How can you write what you just wrote and ask me that question?" he asks, pouring my wine. "We should be talking of love."

With any luck I will not have to write another bedroom scene involving my husband. That done, I can turn my attention to world affairs.

"Those were Basque cops," Mulvaney insists. "They knew exactly who he was."

Mulvaney-true, I think.

"We were there to do an interview, not make an arrest," he continues.

"The guy killed the premier of Spain!"

"He killed a Franco crony. A big crony. You said it yourself. You even wrote it."

"Mulvaney, have you ever heard of the legal system?"

He is ignoring me. "If you look behind some of these other guys, the guys who only want their own countries back, the ones who don't want to take over the world, then you'll find, in some, a core of decency."

"Mulvaney, somebody is going to shoot *you*!"

"Sometimes you'll find humor and a zest for what is good in life. You will find retribution that may be deserved and is certainly comprehensible. And you'll find competence, too. You'll find Nelson Mandela."

"You'll find Winnie. And it is cheap to use Nelson Mandela to defend the IRA."

"Nelson Mandela also killed people. Look, who was the first person ETA killed this century?"

"Mulvaney, I don't keep track of these things like you do."

"It was that Manzanas guy."

"Apples?"

"Literally, yes. But in real life, nothing that sweet. He was the Gestapo's man in San Sebastián. He helped them get the Jews fleeing France."

"Old business."

"If your mother heard that, she'd smack you. Old business it's not. The Spanish government gave the guy a posthumous medal, saying he was a super cop murdered by ETA. But that's all they're saying. ETA was pretty pissed about it."

"Good," I said.

"There you go."

"There I go what?"

"Glorifying assassins."

I'll need a second book just to explain the first. "You can't be right about this without also being wrong."

"Hence screwball's the way to go."

"There is no way I am going to write a screwball comedy and put Tiananmen Square in it," I say.

"Unless you're talking about the way they came up with their official body count," he replies.

CHAPTER 31

Partition

Midmorning, days later, I was still doing the very things I had vowed never to do again with Mulvaney.

Some of them more than once.

Did it count if you did them in Spain?

The bellboy banged on the door but we didn't answer. He announced he was leaving the mail outside.

After Mulvaney fell back asleep, I retrieved two packages from Ronkonkoma. One had blank reporters' notebooks in it.

Leisure Suit had successfully FedExed supplies overseas. Maybe he *was* qualified to be foreign editor.

The other had been half opened by customs to reveal a

bundled stack of upside-down *Newsday*s from earlier in the week.

Ah, I thought.

Without scissors, I pulled at the plastic ties to loosen them and slid out a newspaper. A small box on the front page read "Former Huntington Bookstore Owner Details Spanish Premier Assassination in '73. See page 3."

It was true. Good play was as good as good sex.

I took a moment for humility. What, really, had we done except get a confession on a decade-old murder in a foreign country that was no longer a world power? Lucky for us a whale hadn't hit the beach lately.

Forget humility. We had gotten a confession on a decade-old murder. And we had delved into the psyche of an assassin. Quickly, I turned the page, eager to see my name.

And Mulvaney's.

No matter what happened to our so-called romance, it would be nice to show a double byline to the grandchildren we weren't going to have.

But all the byline said was "by Jim Mulvaney."

I assessed how much I'd drunk the night before.

By Jim Mulvaney.

I tried to stay calm. Maybe they'd given me a tagline at the end of the story, which, although not great, would be better than nothing.

"Continued on page 32."

The jump to our story was buried underneath a short about Nassau County Comptroller Peter King and his plans for yet another trip to attempt to bring peace to Northern Ireland.

Lots of Peter King but no tagline.

Alongside the jump was the sidebar. "Mysteries of Spanish Bathrooms," by Jim Mulvaney and Barbara Fischkin.

Fuck.

It sounded like I went to Spain with Mulvaney to write a home-decorating story. And needed his help to do even that.

This was worse than Pamplona without bulls.

Much worse.

I shook him awake. He pulled me back into bed. I grabbed the blanket from him.

"Mulvaney," I said, "not now. Not ever again!"

"What?"

My head nodded toward the pile of *Newsday*s.

Slowly he stood, then stopped. Mulvaney's dread, like most things about him, is selective, informed when it needs to be, even when he is naked. He looked at me. Blue eyes. "I am hoping," he said, "that you are trying to tell me that Leisure Suit was a jerk and identified Xanti by his real name."

We'd had to cough that up to the editor. He had promised to leave it out of the story, although he'd told us that if he ever got subpoenaed he would tell all, especially if they threatened him with expulsion from Suffolk County.

Mulvaney picked up the package, pulled out a paper, opened to the page. "Oh shit," he said apologetically. "I swear I dictated your byline." He put his arm around me.

I pulled it off.

Facts: He had romanced me, screwed me, then really screwed me.

Conclusion: He used his quirkiness to charm. But deep down he was a creep.

•   •

We flew back to Dublin in silence, hailed a taxi without making eye contact. Mulvaney asked the driver to drop him off on O'Connell Street in front of the post office, the site of the Easter Uprising of 1916, the beginning of the Irish Revolution.

"Partition," he said, coldly referring to the ending of that particular chapter of Irish history. "You stay south. I'll go north."

He took his doctor's bag from the trunk and leaned through the open window, handing me a tangled clump of Irish punts, presumably to pay the driver.

I pushed his hand away.

"I put your byline on the story," he said. "It fell off, so you blame me. If you think I am that petty, we are done."

"Bylines," I said, "are not like towels hanging on a fence. They are not like Band-Aids. They are not like Humpty Dumpty."

I rolled the window down farther and eyed his crotch. "They are not like balls. They do not fall off."

I sped away, alone in the taxi. What a jerk! He'd just broken up with me because *he'd* done something unforgivable. And he still needed to use Irish history as a crutch.

Most people would say "I'm leaving."

Mulvaney had to first reenact a battle fought almost seven decades earlier, a battle that eventually led to the division of Ireland into the Republic in the South and the six counties that made up the North. A solution that only brought on more war.

Our troubles *were* like Ireland's. We had periods of uneasy peace, fragile cease-fires, proclamations of unity, compromise, subterfuge, and then bang, bang, war again.

It had taken a lot of work to understand Mulvaney and metaphors. But I'd only gotten it half right. He didn't get metaphors but he did make them happen.

I've always been an overzealous fan of dry cleaning. Well-pressed clothing wrapped in plastic sends me into spasms of bliss. This condition has only escalated in the years since I've known Mulvaney. I use dry cleaning to blot out the sloppiness inherent in marriage. I also use it to help me accept the inevitable.

"Name?"

The suits and blouses are tallied and piled. The clerk's pen is perched at the top of the bill, waiting.

"Mrs. Mulvaney," I say.

Everywhere else my name is still Barbara Fischkin. It is only at the dry cleaners that I say I am Mrs. Mulvaney. I have been Mrs. Mulvaney at dry cleaners on four continents.

Perhaps I just want to shift the blame for my dirty, wrinkled clothes onto Mulvaney and his ancestors. Every wife needs some private way to get back at her husband for his sins, both real and imagined.

ACT THREE

CHAPTER 32

Message Pending

A thick, white card scribbled in fountain pen was under my door at the Kilronan House. Colm wanted me to go back to Paris with him. "Sam Beckett," he wrote, "slept in his bathtub until Nora took pity and brought him a proper mattress and frame...."

I'd asked him into the Irish bed of a Joycean character.

Now he was asking me into the Joycean bed of an Irish character.

Would Beckett watch?

No wonder I didn't know what I wanted.

• •

My mother had sent a clip from *Ms.* magazine. Two paragraphs on excessive strip searches of women prisoners in Armagh. "An interview for Jim to do," she'd noted in the margin.

I hid in the Kilronan House for days. Then I went to pubs without phones. I didn't answer my own.

At Toner's on Baggot Street, the cracked mirror behind the bar had fogged and the men in it all looked familiar. Three times I thought I saw Mulvaney.

At last, a woman appeared. She held up a long strand of black hair.

"Blondes have more fun," she mouthed.

The story of my life.

"They have more fun because they don't have to fly to Ireland *just to get a drink.* . . ."

I turned. "Claire," I said, and started to cry.

It really was her.

She ordered two glasses of Guinness and handed me a linen handkerchief with shamrocks, the kind they sell to tourists at the airport. "It's better than you think," she said. "At least you don't have a job."

"He finally fired me."

She nodded. "He really liked the Basque story. But then you disappeared."

I had.

"I'll fix it," she said. "Just give me something Mulvaney can't do."

Suddenly I felt great, like my hard, old self. "They're torturing women in Armagh Prison," I said.

Claire sighed impatiently. "I said one Mulvaney *can't* do."

"You want him asking Irish females why they don't like to take their clothes off?"

Claire, who really had come for just a drink, needed to get back to New York. To prolong the visit, I rode with her to the airport.

"It was a sorry chain of events," she said. The byline question. I wished she hadn't brought *that* up. "It started when the Men got a computer nerd to help them finish *Naked Returns the Stranger*. Well, you know what bad drunks computer nerds are..."

A concept I could imagine...

"They took him to the Ground Round, plied him with Long Island Iced Teas. Finally, he spit up a way for them to use Message Pending under disguised identities...."

Our taxi stopped short at Departures and a string of rosary beads jangled around the rearview mirror. So much for the illusion of nonsectarianism.

Claire leaned over and paid the driver with a few new, smooth punts. "This, of course, was just what the Men, particularly the Non-*Naked* Men, wanted to hear. Having had a taste of sex writing, they wanted more of it. They wanted it more dangerous, too."

The taxi driver coughed; Claire gave him a dismissive wave. "And now they had the tools to do it. And instead of writing together, they wanted to compete. Whoever sent the dirtiest anonymous note to the highest-ranking *Newsday* executive would win."

Clearly the Men, all of them, needed to get out of Long Island.

"Unfortunately the publisher stopped it. But not before he

came all the way to Garden City to tell us that he had never felt so beloved. There wasn't an orifice of his, or a backroom in Ronkonkoma, left out of the picture."

"Darlin'!" the Catholic taxi driver said.

Claire kissed me, opened the door, got out. What did this have to do with Mulvaney?

She peered in through the open back window. "All those Messages Pending crashed the system. That was the night you reported from Pamplona and wrote from San Sebastián. You guys did a great job, but back in Ronkonkoma the place was a mess."

She handed me a printout—with a Pamplona dateline. "I made this before the crash." This was, indeed, the way stories looked right after reporters filed them, before they were formatted to be published.

"I had to type some of the stories back into the system," she called back as she ran to her plane. "I'm the one who left your byline off."

Claire then disappeared into the Irish fog.

The printout had my name on it.

Colm was not at the Kilkenny Design Centre. If I wandered inside the gates of Trinity, I might find his office. I could finally see the Book of Kells, too. My second time in Dublin and I'd had yet to see *The Book*. Who'd had time for illuminated manuscripts?

I bought a cappuccino and read the *Irish Press* instead. It was the most Republican of the Dublin dailies, and it made a big deal over the impending burial of three IRA men in Belfast, purposely delayed until Peter King's visit. King, who loved drama as long as it didn't happen on Long Island, had arranged to arrive in Belfast on Orangeman's Day. That was when Protestants in the North celebrated their centuries-old victory at the Battle of the Boyne—and the legacy of Oliver Cromwell—with more verve than anyone at the Huntington Yacht Club could ever imagine.

The IRA men, caught digging up a cache of guns, had been shot on sight, an echo of what had happened to Jim Mulvenna years before. The other Jim Mulvenna.

How, I wondered, did Peter King explain the convolution of events like this funeral to his constituents at Jones Beach?

I thought of the Claddagh ring, back in its paper bag. Should I throw it away?

Or sell it?

If I kept this up, I might need the money.

Love, Friendship, Loyalty. Here in the land of poets they couldn't come up with anything less sentimental? How had Mulvaney managed to give this to me without being a cliché himself? He had taken the ring out of a crumpled bag. Most men would have handed over a box tied with a ribbon.

"You're not going to throw it away, are you?" he had asked.

He was so sure of himself. He'd gone to war. He talked to people who killed other people. My mother said he wrote like an old man. She meant that he was confident. He was always confident about his stories. The ones he wrote, the ones he told, and the ones he made up, especially those. He acted confident about me.

But that's what it was, an act. *"You're not going to throw it away, are you?"* What was it about Mulvaney besides the blue eyes?

"Hullo. I'm Jim Mulvaney." He'd walked up to me in the newsroom. I did not walk up to him. Then he'd cooled down. But then he'd followed me. Mulvaney would never admit that

he had done more than follow a story into what was, coincidentally, my parents' shul. I finished my coffee, stared at a swirl of froth lining the bottom of the fashionable white mug. Colm would never follow me anywhere. He would wait for me. But if I did not show up, he would not try to find me. He would shrug his shoulders, leave for Paris, and get a cancan girl to sleep with him in the bed Nora Joyce brought for Samuel Beckett.

Why would a man who had your mother kidnap you and bring you to him in Northern Ireland care who got the byline?

The next day I called Claire in Ronkonkoma. Had she ever been here?

"The professor reacts," I said. "Answering a question is easier than asking one."

"That he can't ask questions," Claire said, "does not make a man unattractive to me."

"You must be on deadline; you're changing sides."

"Just making sure you know what's attractive to *you*."

"It is more than mildly intriguing to wonder if there is something I can do to rattle Colm." But it is not, I thought sadly to myself, the same as watching the effect you have already had on someone who is at ease with the world but not necessarily with you.

"The prison—can you get in?"

How hard could it be to get *into* prison? "This isn't about Mulvaney," I said.

"Don't forget the Long Island angle!" she replied, and hung up.

Public retribution in marriage is not a bad thing either. Mulvaney disagrees.

He may say we are still married because there is always another story but I say it's because there is always another argument. He thinks we can be at peace because I am finished with Colm. I, though, reserve the right, years from now, to blame Mulvaney for making me dump a perfectly compelling fictional character.

If we accept marriage, we accept it with its flaws.

Even if it means he might throw Marsha back in my face.

CHAPTER 33

Doomed

Stormont Castle in Belfast, the baronial seat of Northern Ireland's provincial government, had once been a simple Georgian house. Now, though, it was awash in turrets and griffins, the result of an ostentatious remodeling that had milked its Catholic tenant farmers dry. Outside, around the city, bonfires raged and the Pope burned in effigy.

A third-tier, pimply British PR man met me in the vast, empty lobby. He did not look happy about being the last one at the office on the eve of Northern Ireland's most important Protestant holiday.

I'd timed this hoping for a rube who might say yes.

"Sure, you can tour the prison," he told me.

I cheered to myself. "Tomorrow, okay?" Who said war zones had to be inefficient?

He grinned and put a hand to his splotchy face. "Just make sure you don't interview anyone."

This could put a damper on my story.

"We are doing you an enormous favor," he assured me. "We generally do not let media into the Northern Irish prisons at all."

"How come?" I asked, feigning absolute curiosity.

Troubled, he paused. "These places are filled with our prisoners."

"Yes?"

"And we don't think our prisoners should be exposed to the media."

"Protecting your prisoners from the ruthlessness of the media is very enlightened."

"I mean, it's not for us to allow them the platform to expound their views."

"On how they feel about taking off their clothes?"

His face blushed beyond its spotty red. He cleared his throat. "To expound Provisional or Republican propaganda," he said.

"So you'd let me in to see *Protestant* women who are political prisoners?"

"Hard to tell," he said. "We don't have any."

On Orangeman's Day, downstairs at the Armagh Arms Bed and Breakfast, Protestant men surrounded me. This was their day, an unabashed show of Cromwellian pride. Later, in nearby Drumcree, they would march purposely through a Catholic neighborhood, instigating the locals, many of whom were no angels either.

Armagh Prison itself was a two-hundred-year-old brown-stone fortress that loomed at the end of a long park. Impressive for a holding pen, even if it wasn't as splendid as Stormont. The large woman at the gate, a low-level Amazonian, smiled into the morning clouds, waiting for the inevitable downpour.

"I am here to visit my cousin," I said, handing her the worn slip of notebook paper Mulvaney had given me in another time, in another city. This was not the way I had wanted to get in.

"Ach," she said, as she opened her jacket and fondled a pistol, gleaming and silver in a holster around her waist. "From America? Aye? Me cousin's in Massapequa."

I rejoiced. A Long Island angle!

"Massapequa's beautiful." I forced my eyes away from her gun. Had I ever been to Massapequa?

"Aye," she said, her eyes dreamy. "Dew yew know how I can get meself a wee visa?"

I gazed hard at the stone walls. "But not as pretty as here," I said.

"Aye," she said, nodding. "And yer name?" She put pencil to clipboard. "Missus what?"

I froze. What were the chances that Barbara Fischkin would have a cousin in Armagh Prison?

"My name..." I gulped, feeling like one of the imposters on *I've Got a Secret*. "My name is Mrs. Mulvaney."

"Brilliant!" said the guard, although that was not my assessment.

•   •

Mulvaney's Alleged Cousin greeted me looking like she worked in a department store. "Nice," I said, admiring her cinched purple knit dress, sheer nylons, and delicate velvet pumps.

"It's because I'm a political prisoner, not a wee ord'nary, daysent criminal," she emphasized.

We sat in a classroom, at tiny desks. She offered me a tin of biscuits and tea she poured from a thermos decorated with small stick-on daisies. Unlike Xanti, she admitted to nothing. Easier to confess, I thought, when the cops don't have you— or want you.

"They say I was in a house where explosives were made and that I was in a convoy of cars carrying them," she told me. But without elaboration. She couldn't possibly be Mulvaney's cousin.

I listened with what I hoped was a reporter's ear, which was supposed to mean I was on nobody's side.

The PR man did not *want* to understand why the least-privileged citizens of his country were so angry. Yet the Alleged Cousin had tried to kill people. I didn't doubt that some of the women they strip-searched were innocent. But not this one.

An hour later, I walked out of Armagh Prison knowing I'd have to tell its story deadpan. Here are the terrifying things some of these women did. Here are the terrifying things none of them can stand. Down the road, at a small tearoom, I ordered a pot and began scribbling. Who *were* these women?

Mothers, young girls, fifty-year-old women, women with

black lingerie that got confiscated because the prison said it was an IRA color. The guards even searched women who had just had babies, their breasts dripping with milk.

"Like most security, the strip searches are random," the Alleged Cousin had told me. "You don't know the night before if they are going to make you take off your clothes in the morning or not. They do no internal searches but they get to our insides in other ways. They look at you steadily, comment on your hair—and I don't mean the hair on your head. Remember, these people are our captors. They decide for how long we stand naked. There's that old enmity, that old hatred: 'We have you where we want you.'"

She was a vital, young woman. But how long would that last? I thought of Amalia, worn and separated from her young daughter. Was a Basque Republic worth it? Did Suzie McBreeze keep a couch full of guns because she wanted a free Ireland? Or to avenge her husband and son? The Alleged Cousin had been a little girl the first time she saw Protestants kill one of her neighbors, Catholic like her. Her brother, like Suzie's son, went to prison as a teenager after he burned up a bus.

All these people simply wanted to be who they were, without suffering any harm. To pledge allegiance to Euskadi, instead of Spain. To work in Northern Ireland and call yourself a Catholic.

But all these people had guns and bombs.

There. I could say it. I could report it out. But could I figure it out? Could I feel it, if it wasn't my own story?

"Yew the Yank who's been in the prison?" A large woman in a guard uniform loomed over me. I closed my notebook, hoping she would think it was a tourist's log.

Without waiting for an answer, she sat. Her thick arms rested on the table. I slipped the notebook into my knapsack.

She wore a waist holster with a gleaming silver gun. "Mrs. Mulvaney?"

"Miss Mulvaney."

"Yew related to that American reporter who lives in Andytown?"

"No," I said. It was true.

"But yew'r American, too?"

I nodded.

She stood to leave. "American women don't mind taking off their clothes. So watch what yew tell people."

From the pay phone at a bank, I called Claire, who accepted the charges but displayed no sympathy.

"Scared by a prison *matron*? When'd you become such a wimp?"

The Orangeman parade was about to explode. "Get there!" she insisted.

"How?" I asked her, still shook.

"What is wrong with you? Do whatever the locals do. It's Northern Ireland. Hijack a car, fergodsakes!"

Mulvaney, she said, could use some help.

I took a bus to Drumcree. The closer we got, the louder the drums banged. From the back window, I saw a line of men in drab black suits and bowler hats turning the corner, marching perpendicular to the bus. They had white gloves, white hair. Even the hair of the young men was white. Their skin was dry, translucent. Each one looked like his own kind of ghost.

But there was color in their politics. Their own color. Orange, not green. Fringed orange shawls, draped over shoulders.

Another line followed, then another, until the parade grew into an endless white mass punctuated by orange, with drumsticks flapping eerily in the wind.

"FTP?" I said, reading the letters off a drum. "What's that, a football team?"

"No such luck, darlin'," the bus driver said. "It stands for 'Fuck the Pope.'"

He opened the door and motioned for me to step down. "Enjoy the parade. Yew'r not Catholic, are yew?"

The street filled with more bowler hats, drums, shawls. Behind me, a row house door opened, spewing out teenagers with shaved heads, some punctuated by isolated tufts of spiky hair dyed orange. Skinheads.

Warriors with cricket bats, they followed their leader and crowded next to me on the sidewalk.

"Fookin' teague!" one of them screamed. The boys raised their bats higher and turned to me as if they might pounce. Great, they thought I *was* Catholic.

"No, there's a fookin' teague marchin'!" the outraged skinhead leader cried out.

In the midst of the Orangemen, I saw a swirl of plaid. It was taking notes.

If only he had worn the tuxedo . . .

"Get the fooking teague!" the skinhead leader ordered.

The boys, bats flashing, stormed the parade line. Mulvaney, who was supposed to be covering these troubles, was now inciting more of his own. I grabbed the shoulder of a marcher who passed by me.

"They can't beat him," I shouted, still not thinking they would. "He's an American reporter." I sounded like my mother.

The marcher pulled my hand off him, pushed me to the ground, and kept walking.

The boys circled their prey. I screamed. I heard wood crack.

Then, slowly, too slow, behind the sticks, a flash of white and orange turned into a tall, paunchy bear of a man. He plucked the skinhead leader from the circle, held him by his collar.

The marchers stopped. The drums got quiet.

"You do not go after this bloke!"

It was Ian Paisley, Northern Ireland's most famous Protestant extremist. No worse than the IRA in what he encouraged. No better. But nowhere near as popular in America. Was that because he was too obvious with his hatred, prejudice, fire and brimstone? Or was it because Protestants from Ulster had come to America too long ago?

His voice boomed like an angry preacher.

"Anyone who lays a finger on this man will answer to me."

The skinheads loosened their circle. Mulvaney's face bled but his eyes blazed as he walked toward me.

"Where's your T-Bird?" I asked, hoping for a quick getaway.

"I took the bus," he said. "Doncha remember what you said to me about driving and doomed Long Islanders?"

"Jim Mulvenna?" A silver gun was poised an inch from Mulvaney's ear, held in the black-gloved hand of a uniformed RUC man.

"Jim Mulvenna is dead," Mulvaney said, his eyes a miraculous, mischievous blue. "Buried with the Provos."

Without even a smile, the RUC man shoved Mulvaney into the back of a car that sped off as the door shut behind them.

As soon as Mulvaney was gone, I missed him.

"Are you happy now?" I ask my husband.

"At least I was tender when they carted you off."

"A slight improvement," he says.

"Don't get used to it. That was the last bit of mush I am putting in this book."

"It's the first bit of mush you've put in the book, and it's barely mush at all. It's barely a sentence. It took a whole book for you to say you might miss me if I went to prison."

"It's a well-placed, tender sentence. The best expressions of love are short."

I get a long blue stare in response.

What I should have written when they carted him off to prison is this: Why do I always like men better when they become unattainable?

CHAPTER 34

Expectations

Something with long red hair drove up in a generic California convertible, an impractical car for a place where the sun never shone.

"Need a lift?" Marsha McCain asked.

A surfboard decorated in green, orange, and white, the colors of the Irish flag, stuck out from her open trunk. She slithered toward the passenger side, stretched her skinny arm, and opened the door. I looked for a Claddagh ring. She didn't have one.

I had no idea where the RUC had taken Mulvaney.

"You better drive fast," I said to Marsha McCain. "It's a long way to the American consulate."

When we got there, we were greeted by an iron gate and a heavy chain. Marsha slapped her head like a beach bunny who had suddenly remembered there are no waves in Nebraska. "Closed for Orangeman's Day," she said.

Diplomacy, I felt, should have its limits.

My red-haired companion did not know where the Consul General lived or drank, confirming her own status as a mildly attractive but ineffectual human being.

I asked Marsha to drop me off at Owenvarragh Park. If anyone could find a high-ranking American on his day off, it was Suzie McBreeze.

Her house was unlocked. But nobody was there.

Peter King, I remembered, was making an appearance at Milltown Cemetery.

I plopped on the couch, glad to feel no lumps. The first time Mulvaney left me, I had said I hoped that he would rot in a foreign prison. But I didn't mean it. I didn't imagine him on a dirt floor surrounded by rats, or even transvestites. I hadn't wished interrogators or torturers on him. All I did was whisper that Mulvaney was the kind of guy who *should* be locked up. And now, here I was in a small house off the Andersonstown Road about to search the Belfast yellow pages for a human rights specialist.

I got up and dialed Pier 92 instead. Easier to find an Irish lawyer in Rockaway. As a waiter answered, I heard Suzie on the front steps and held the door open for her. Without blinking, she clumped past me into the living room and turned on a *Dynasty* rerun, an attempt, I assumed, to assuage her political sorrows.

"Yer woman Crystal . . . ach aye . . . her heart is true," she said, dabbing her eyes with a Kleenex.

I couldn't stand it.

A bottle of tonic sat on a faded patch of carpet remnant. Next to it stood the white canvas bag Suzie had taken to Mother's Night at the Felons Club.

I finished the call and sat down again, next to her, hoping a momentary lack of drama might help me think. Then I felt the couch go hard.

Damn it. The guns were still there. Was that why they had arrested Mulvaney?

She took two glasses from a small side table, poured tonic, dipped the glass into her white bag.

"Single or double?" she asked.

"Suzie! This is your house!" She nodded, handed me the glass, and I gulped. "Gin is one thing you don't have to hide."

"Ach aye." She laughed. Without taking her eyes off John Forsythe, she lifted the liquor bottle from her bar bag and set it next to the tonic, a Belfast still life on that dreadful carpet. "Living with deception becomes habitual," she said casually, still not looking me in the eye.

"Suzie, why do you do it?"

"Shh, it's the good part."

I threw my glass on the floor.

Surprised, she looked at me.

"Suzie, they arrested Mulvaney."

She stood and flipped the television off. "They lifted our Jim? Whatever fer?"

I stood, too, and looked back at the couch. "You probably know better than I do."

A ray of light shot through the door.

Suzie's daughters. "Mummy, we want our tea," Bridget squeaked.

Suzie put down her glass. "Our Jim's been lifted."

The girls stopped, turned, and went solemnly to their rooms. A drill they'd rehearsed. The floor banged. The noise was softer than soldiers throwing mattresses but just as purposeful. I heard a loud snap, the clasp of a hard suitcase.

Suzie looked me up and down and straight in the eye. "I was not stupid," she said, then marched toward her kitchen. "After the Brits came, I got rid of them."

She returned with a knife and slit the couch. "There aren't any there," she said calmly.

Like Armagh Prison and the Alleged Cousin, like Gerry Adams and Danny Morrison, like Xanti and Amalia, like Ian Paisley, I tried to tally up Suzie.

Like Mulvaney, too.

She was a gunrunner who accepted dole checks from the very people she plotted to overthrow. If she was not on the run herself, it was only because she hadn't been caught. Even her own comrades had to put up with her shenanigans. Suzie was a Provo who wouldn't even buy a shot of Provo gin.

But she had taken in Mulvaney, not knowing if she'd get anything out of him. She knew he would write stories. But what kind of stories? She did not insist he take her side. Suzie believed it was more important to make sure the story was told than to direct it herself. And she'd recognized the tenuous connections between my mother's life and her own, not an easy leap across cultures and decades.

Now she put the knife down, ran upstairs, checked her daughters, ran down again with four identical gift boxes, one piled atop another. She opened one and showed me the electric blanket inside.

"Jimmy Mulvenna brought these to us when he moved in. But we couldna get used to 'em. Too many years cold."

She looked me in the eye again. "Fer sure someone wanted to teach yer Jim a lesson."

"Hundreds of people," I agreed.

"Mebbe thousands," Suzie said, her own eyes dancing a jig. "But not me."

It was after six, very dark. Rain, the pouring rain that should have fallen in Northern Ireland all along, finally streamed down. In the kitchen the mahogany cabinet was askew. Past it, in Mulvaney's room, still a mess, the garbage heap lay intact under his bed. I heard the door slam shut; Suzie and the girls were gone. In the hallway the phone rang. I hadn't seen the doctor's bag. He was going to have a hard time being a doctor without it.

I ran back out.

"Unfortunately the princess phone in Mulvaney's cell does not take international calls." Claire's voice prickled over the line. I could hear the Gloomroom's other telephones ringing off its desks. "The PR man in the Northern Ireland office was ever so helpful when he explained that they arrested Mulvaney after he helped *his wife* sneak into Armagh Prison."

Silence.

"Can't you even go on an unauthorized vacation without getting into trouble? They searched his room. About that, though, they are *not* talking."

I looked at the front door and now saw that the lock had been broken. The Brits must have been here while Suzie was at the IRA funeral.

"Leisure Suit says he'll never let a foreign correspondent out of Suffolk County again."

I hung up the phone and screamed.

Is this the secret to Mulvaney's success?

That people take one look at him and expect him to misbehave?

Then, when he does, they congratulate themselves on their insight.

What they really want to hear, though, is that he was the kid who got detention.

When Mulvaney's parents moved from Queens to Garden City, they believed it would be the Real Long Island. Or what Long Island wanted to be anyway. White and Planned.

Mulvaney, though, was White and Unplanned. It wasn't long before he convinced his numerous new friends to take the golf carts at the country club joyriding at three a.m. They ruined the greens.

"Good practice for driver's ed," he explained.

The first time he went to college, he got kicked out.

It was only Thomas Pynchon—as hard as this is to believe—that got him back in. But I have finally identified it as a true-true Mulvaney tale. Well, it's as true-true as a Mulvaney tale gets.

"I told you you needed more about my childhood," he says.

As for me, I just let everyone think that I really did kill my kindergarten teacher.

CHAPTER 35
How Many People Does It Take to Free a Mulvaney?

My mother walked off the plane at Aldergrove, waving an aging paperback copy of Leon Uris's *Exodus*. Her other hand was hooked through the elbow of a fellow traveler, a weary Protestant businessman.

"The Brits did the same thing in Palestine," my mother said, shaking the book in his face as she hunched her shoulders to keep her large psychedelic carry-on from slipping off.

Carefully, as if she herself were a bomb set to detonate Belfast, the man extricated himself from her hold and scooted away. My mother shrugged and threw her arms around me. "You didn't think I was going to have you spring poor Jim Mulvaney all by yourself?"

"How's Dad?"

Suddenly her Peter Max bag leaped, as if by itself, off her shoulder.

"Asta," she explained. "As you remember, she loves Jim Mulvaney."

My mother had now smuggled a dog into Northern Ireland.

"Why didn't you just declare her?" Why didn't she just leave her home?

"Too inconvenient," my mother said. "In rabies-free Northern Ireland, all newcomer dogs must be quarantined for six months. She'll be fine. She's on Valium. Just needs another dose."

Peaceable mutts? Here? The bigger question was could we do a prisoner swap? Queen Asta for Mulvaney?

"Maybe she'll sleep through the Europa," I said, as my mother's bag yelped drowsily.

"It was very comfortable last time," my mother assured me. "Particularly for a hotel under siege."

While my mother unpacked her dog, I went to the hotel bar, where I found the Real Mulvaney drinking a martini and chatting up the cocktail waitress. He had flown into Dublin, driven north on what was for him the wrong side of the road, and now, in the thick of happy hour in Belfast, an oxymoron if ever there was one, he looked as if he had never left Pier 92.

"Gin and tonic," I said as I climbed onto the stool next to his.

I spotted my mother on the staircase, Queen Opium Bow-Wow resting comfortably, and illegally, in her arms for all of Northern Ireland to see.

As they made their way to the bar, the Real Mulvaney bent his head in deference to the royal couple, then took my mother's hand and kissed it.

"My *machetunim!*" he declared. His Yiddish was as imprecise as his assumption. One female in-law: *machetayneste.* For *machetunim,* in Felshtin at least, you needed two or more. Dogs don't count.

"She is no such thing!" I said to the Real Mulvaney, spilling gin on my Paris sweater.

Mulvaney couldn't even get arrested without convening a family reunion. Mine—and his. Didn't most people become foreign correspondents to get away from their relatives?

Queen Asta, suddenly aroused, yelped, jumped, and ran, dashing my hopes she'd remain drugged forever. My mother ran after her. I ran after my mother. Losing track of Ida Fischkin in Belfast was not, as I'd learned the last time, a good idea. The Real Mulvaney watched from the archway of the bar, looking as if he knew the truth. We could need counsel for the dog, too.

At the registration desk, Queen Asta jumped between two men in American trench coats, one tall, the other short, and barked a chorus. Startled, one of the men turned, bent to pet the dog. As his coat fell open, I spotted a white carnation.

"Gary Ackerman!" I said over the mutt's yelps. "You've come to free Mulvaney."

He twisted his face into a sardonic grin. "Actually, I was hoping to bring peace to Northern Ireland."

"Very funny," said the taller man, Peter King. Ecstatic, Queen Asta jumped into his arms and licked his face. So the mutt was a Republican. It figured. As the dog slavered, the

Real Mulvaney bounced out from the bar archway and into the arms of both politicians. All of them, including the dog, congratulated one another, as if the true heroes of the Irish Revolution had come home.

"Your son was supposed to introduce me to Ian Paisley," Gary Ackerman complained.

The Real Mulvaney nodded. "Who says he won't?"

"Paisley loves Mulvaney," King agreed. "He says Mulvaney's the only American who has ever written fairly about the Prods."

This, I hoped, was not their entire defense. It wasn't even true. "This is between Mulvaney and the Brits," I reminded them. "Who cares what Ian Paisley thinks?"

"We might," said Peter King, Long Island's most prominent Irish Republican.

My husband is morose. This is worse than having him under arrest. "Where are you heading with this?" he asks. "The book needs closure."

Before I became a fiction writer, he never used words like "closure." "We are working up to some core ideas," I say. "Truth is the sum of many fragmented but necessary small truths—and small lies. How they all work together is an individual truth."

"Don't make this a self-help book."

"Mulvaney," I say. "No one would ever accuse it of that. But the individual truth of this book is that no story is ever your own story. Every story you tell is someone else's story. True-true doesn't exist."

"The book is over, then," he says.

"The book is never over. This may be a book about a simple romance. But no romance is ever simple. They all begin like this. And none of them ever end."

I have, I realize, just committed to writing a sequel.

CHAPTER 36

Not Without Me

Nobody was bombing the Europa. But I still couldn't sleep.

"You should take a Valium," my mother offered.

We wouldn't be able to see Mulvaney until the following morning. I examined my roommates. My mother and her dog.

"Hand them over," I agreed.

As she did, Queen Asta emitted a growl so filled with long-standing animosity that I popped two.

"I don't know what to do with Mulvaney," I said to myself.

"You may see," my mother commented, "that you have no choice except to marry him. It may regularize his situation."

"A steamroller might regularize his situation."

She pulled down the blanket on her side of the bed.

"Mother, you always said it would kill you if I didn't marry someone Jewish."

"People become Jewish," my mother said, not for the first time.

She still did not comprehend the worldwide havoc that would ensue if Mulvaney, who already believed he was chosen by God, converted. Then he'd have five-thousand-plus years of history to back up his overblown opinion of himself.

"He's perfect for you," she said. "You are two equally contentious, difficult, and occasionally delightful human beings, although he is more often delightful than you are." She tucked the yawning Queen Asta between us. I lifted the mutt and moved it closer to her.

I yawned now, too. "I can't marry him when he's under arrest."

"You can do anything you set your mind to do, dear," my mother said.

I hadn't meant to oversleep on the morning we were going to free Mulvaney. The fire alarms woke me. Then the phone. My mother was nowhere to be seen.

"Hiya, toots!"

"Daddy?" I muttered through the clanging. "Where are you?"

"Downstairs."

Was this a dream, or a nightmare?

Or worse.

Machetunim.

"I'm having an Ulster Fry with Pete and Gary!"

Eggs, bacon, sausage, and fried soda bread. A meal that should come with your own Christiaan Barnard.

"Delicious!" my father reported.

I sat up in bed.

"Pete King tried to tell me it was kosher, but I know a charming liar when I see one."

I asked my father why he was in Belfast.

"Barbara, I'm surprised you would ask. Who sprung *me* when I needed *him*?" My father said he would have come even sooner if it hadn't been "Take a Chance on Saturday Nite." "Now get down here or you'll miss Long Kesh Prison."

Did he think he was on a European bus tour for Jewish senior citizens?

I ran out the front door of the chaotic hotel just as my parents, Queen Asta, Gary Ackerman, Peter King, and the Real Mulvaney were getting into a taxi. Safe in the commodious back, I pulled down a stool, breathed in the comforting smell of my father's Phillies Panatelas, kissed him, and glared at my mother.

"Nice try, Mom," I said. "You should have used more Valium."

"It was for your own good, dear," my mother replied. "Just don't mess anything up by talking."

"Mother, I happen to have a bit more experience than you do when it comes to Northern Irish prisons."

"And if you hadn't insisted on doing that story, Jim Mulvaney wouldn't be where he is right now. I don't know why you couldn't have been happy interviewing that perfectly nice carousel man."

How did she know about that?

More important, how long could I keep up a romance with a man in prison? In Albany—when I'd run out of incarcerated senior citizens for my "After Sixty" column—I'd interviewed women who did that, the ones who took buses to the Greene County State Penitentiary twice a month, comparing love letters along the way. Most of them were disenfranchised, woebegone individuals, wives and girlfriends of tinkers or the American equivalent, women who only fell for difficult men.

But at least those difficult men wrote love letters.

I couldn't imagine Mulvaney writing me a love letter from prison. More likely he'd write stories for *Newsday* about his experience in Long Kesh and expect me, or my mother, to read between the lines and surmise that he needed me.

Gary Ackerman turned from his front seat. "How is the egg mayonnaise here?" he asked, changing the subject just in time.

"The best thing you can say about Northern Ireland's egg mayonnaise," I announced, "is that no one in Long Kesh Prison ever pined for it."

The car went silent. I put my hand over my mouth. Soon we might know if that was true.

"But that's just my opinion," I added hastily.

My mother snorted. "My Barbara's opinions shift like the wind. It's because she doesn't have a stable relationship."

"We're not going to Long Kesh," Ackerman said, as if he were surprised I hadn't figured this out. "They are holding him in Stormont Castle."

"Is that good?" I asked. I knew it was. Still, Mulvaney and turrets would not mix well.

"At Stormont, this won't be a real day in court. It will look more like a political negotiation, an international insult, an affront to America and its citizens abroad. At Long Kesh, it would be a bail hearing."

Feeling every bump in the road, I held on tight to my fold-up stool. Across from me, the Real Mulvaney, in a fedora, jotted notes on a yellow legal pad. Finally I could envision the Real Mulvaney as a real attorney. I'd known he'd been a prosecutor and a defense lawyer. But I'd never actually seen him in a courtroom, or a law office. Only on a barstool.

He put down his legal pad and looked me in the eye. His were brown. "Just let Pete and Gary do the talking. If there's anything you want to add, say you need to speak to your attorney outside."

"My attorney?"

"Yes. Me."

"You have a license to practice in Northern Ireland?"

"Small, inconsequential point."

"Don't worry," Peter King said, "the last thing the Northern Ireland Office wants is for Mulvaney to spend any time in Long Kesh. Think of the stories he would find. Think of the stories that would be written *about* him."

Now I *was* worried. He would love that.

"I hope you are not saying that this is any old love story."

He is twisting my words. I should be used to it.

"Mulvaney," I say, "there is not one individual in the world who is like you." This is true-true. I have never met another Jim Mulvaney.

Now his blue eyes smile.

"You've never said that."

What he doesn't know is that I am saying it now just in case I decide never to let him out of prison. I could do that and change my life. I could change my past.

Writing a novel about your husband has its virtues.

But why not end it on a sweet note?

"I've written a whole book—well, almost a whole book—saying there is no one like you." I stop and kiss him on the lips. "And how many women even write books about their husbands?"

"Many," he says. "But they don't admit it."

CHAPTER 37

Castle Arrest

All of us, the dog included, were led out of the Stormont elevator into an immense Georgian reception area with marble columns and a carved ceiling. It resembled nothing as much as the Foreign Affairs ballroom in Dublin. These people all had the same architects. Why couldn't they get along?

"It could use another renovation," my mother offered. "Some updating. Flowered carpeting might make it seem warmer."

Queen Asta yelped in agreement.

How long, I wondered, would I have to wait for someone to arrest that mutt?

A narrow section of the wall popped open, revealing a bare office with a round table. As we entered, the wall slammed shut behind us.

"Mulvaney!"

The sight of him took my breath away. I had to admit it. I could write a whole book saying it didn't, then revise everything with one small gulp for air.

Even better, no one had beat him since the skinheads.

Two soldiers stood close, as if escape was a distinct possibility.

"How are you?" he asked, filling the room with blue.

"How do you think I am?" I snapped.

No way was I going public with my affections at Stormont Castle, the seat of Northern Irish oppression.

The soldiers moved closer to me.

"Great," Mulvaney said. "Go ahead and let everyone know what a bitch you are. Use a man to help *you* get a story. Then leave him in Dublin."

The soldiers moved back toward him.

"Mulvaney, *you* left *me* in Dublin."

"And you stole my story."

"You *gave* me that prison story."

"Only the story. You *took* my name!"

As if I would ever want it.

The door popped open again and in trotted the Northern Irish PR man, followed by his boss, Britain's Secretary for Northern Ireland, a man who never uttered a word anywhere if it had the potential to be quoted in a newspaper.

When the PR man saw me, he shook his head, dug a silver cigarette lighter out from the pocket of his smooth, dark suit, and tapped it on the table. "Mrs. Mulvaney," he said.

I do not speak to anyone in public relations, I told myself, and took a seat between Ackerman and King. At times like this, it's best to put your faith in America.

The door opened, with more reverence this time, and a man carrying a large briefcase entered. He patted the Real Mulvaney on the back. "Mrs. Mulvaney," he said, nodding to me. This was getting tedious. "I'm Mulvaney's solicitor."

Along with a wife who wasn't his wife, Mulvaney now had a lawyer who wasn't his father.

"I despise Catholicism," boomed the next voice in the doorway, and both Ackerman and King gasped. "But I like Mulvaney!" The large, white-haired man tapped his walking stick on the marble floor of Stormont Castle, as if he owned it.

"Reverend Paisley!" A nervous Peter King offered his hand. "It's a start. Mulvaney's a start."

Were they really going to attempt to solve this conflict one Catholic at a time?

Being married to Mulvaney, I approach all refrigerator Post-it notes with trepidation.

"Gone to Hollywood," this one says. "Keep revising."

I return to my own life, otherwise known as "the raw end of the deal."

The agent e-mails to say he is going to Elaine's. He'd like to take me. But he understands. I am writing.

"have red yr book still lik it," he notes. It will, he says, go nicely with "the screnply" that Mulvaney is now presenting to movie moguls on the West Coast.

"Have you been telling your life story?" I ask my wayward husband when he calls from a phone booth on Sunset Boulevard.

"It's not called 'telling,'" he says. "It's called 'pitching.'" He is proud that he knows film-business lingo.

"Like in baseball?" I ask.

"Yep, it's a metaphor."

Hollywood has changed him already.

"Mulvaney," I say, "pitching isn't you. I do not think of you and imagine the precision of a good arm, the focus of a swishing bat, the ballet of a fly ball caught.

"I think you should bowl your story in," I continue, not without rancor. "When I see you, Mulvaney, I see a lead ball hitting a dozen hard objects. I see perilous alleys, rumbling crashes. What about hockey? Or chariot racing? Now, there's a sport that reminds me of you."

Pitching, he insists, is what it will be. And they want it in one sentence.

The next time my husband calls from Hollywood, I suggest he tell the moguls that the screenplay is based on a marriage manual. Surprising how quickly I have embraced the art of misrepresentation. "It's based on a book that tells you how to get married and stay that way."

"Even the agent would have a problem saying that with a straight face," Mulvaney tells me.

I argue my case. Traditional marriage manuals explain how to get and keep the perfect man. But what about all the women who fall in love with deranged human beings and find they have no choice but to marry them? They need a book. A film, too.

How to Get and Keep the Imperfect Male.

"There are more women like me than you think," I say. "Ones who battle their better instincts and lose."

"One sentence." He is adamant.

"Okay, this film shows you how to marry a man with a mess under his bed, including perhaps—but not limited to—a few handguns."

"Staying married is harder than getting married," he says.

No kidding, Mulvaney. Newlyweds, I tell him, should buy platform beds.

And consider aluminum siding.

CHAPTER 38
Silver Linings

The PR man tapped that silver lighter. "As spokesman for the Northern Ireland Office..." He tapped more. Why didn't he just smoke? Or get a gavel? "I am here to charge James Edward Mulvaney Jr. with illegal possession of numerous weapons!"

"What?" I stood.

I should have known. I did know. At Suzie's house. I knew and chose to ignore it.

"Shh," warned the Real Mulvaney.

The PR man's lighter gleamed in my eye. "You arrested him because I went to prison!" I said.

The PR man grinned. "Aye. And then we found a pile of guns under his bed."

How, I wondered, had they found anything in that mess?

Ceremoniously, he fished into the lapel pocket of his cheap polyester suit—couture beyond even Mulvaney—extracted a set of photographs, and slid one across the table. A photograph of a heap of shining silver guns.

"An unauthorized doctor's bag, too," the PR man added, tossing another photo my way.

I looked at Mulvaney. He'd turned so green his eyes weren't blue anymore. So maybe he did do it.

Nah. He was nuts. But he wasn't a gunrunner.

The British Secretary for Northern Ireland whispered into the ear of the PR man.

"Speak, Mulvaney!" the PR man ordered. "Speak for yourself. Unless, of course, you'd prefer me to do it for you."

Mulvaney, graduated now from green to gray, stood hesitantly and launched into an explanation so unlike him that I'd rather our grandchildren didn't know about it.

Mulvaney's stories, especially Mulvaney-true stories, are told with triumph. They are Irish drinking songs with no hangover. Romance with no breakups. Rebel music but only if the rebels win. This was none of those things.

I could see on his face that he imagined he'd never be a reporter again.

Everyone talked at once. The PR man tapped his lighter for order. I turned my head, hoping to focus it on anything that did not shine. But my eyes stopped, instead, at more glare, the silver gun in the prison officer's holster.

I remembered the guns in Suzie's couch.

"Hold it!" I said. "Silver's wrong."

"It's a lovely color, dear," my mother insisted. "And a neutral shade."

"Ida!" my father said.

I watched Mulvaney's pallor disappear. He knew what I knew and tilted his head to the door.

"Uh, outside please," I said to the Real Mulvaney. Then to the others, "I want to speak to our lawyer."

Mulvaney, my Mulvaney, the unreal one, smiled blue.

"He can't practice here," said the boy PR man.

"He can if I authorize him on my behalf," the solicitor argued with magisterial self-importance.

"Have you ever been to Rockaway?" I asked him.

In the ballroom, I gripped the Real Mulvaney's arm. "The guns they say they found are silver. The guns Suzie kept in the couch were black matte."

He nodded. "The bad guys always use matte because they don't glow in the dark."

As far as I was concerned, they were all bad guys. "So who uses silver?"

"People who are supposed to have guns."

"Like cops?"

"Like prison officers," the Real Mulvaney said. "Silver guns are easier to keep. They don't rot like the black ones."

Nothing like imagining a good story and then actually coming up with a fact. And what was that photo of *silver* guns if not a fact? The Brits had planted a pile of silver guns under Mulvaney's bed. Their own guns. Then they'd retrieved them as "evidence."

"Be careful," the Real Mulvaney said. "You could make it worse. Let Pete and Gary handle this. Unless, of course, you think you can prove it."

If only I could imagine an expert witness, one who knew weapons and how to use them. A distinguished academic type, Irish, with connections to all factions in this farce. He would get Mulvaney off and sweep me away to a quiet French restaurant, one that really was in France. Then he'd pour the red wine for me, not as well as Mulvaney but more quietly, with fewer spills, and gently offer me the opportunity to decide between the two of them.

No. He would tell me there was no need to decide. I could have them both.

The key to being a happy woman: Live with true love and an escape route.

In real life the PR man called us back inside and announced that the Northern Irish Secretary intended to arrest me, too, for stealing prison guards' guns and giving them to Mulvaney.

This, I told him, would not improve the romance.

"You've done it now," Mulvaney says. He is back from California, without a deal or a refusal. We know people who've gone on for years like this. It is the same as some marriages.

"This is what every woman wants," he says. "To aggrandize a man in her imagination and make him fall in love with her. Then knock him down so that she can spend the rest of her days telling him he is a failure who has made her life a prison sentence."

"You don't know how it ends," I say.

"It ends with you," he says. "Proving you can't share a story."

True-true: I don't know how it ends either.

But I bet someone in Hollywood has an implausible suggestion.

CHAPTER 39

Can We Get It Annulled?

Ian Paisley stood over Mulvaney and banged his Orangeman's walking stick, hard, on the marble floor of Stormont.

"I saved this young man's life because I believed he was a fair and balanced reporter," he bellowed in his broad Northern Irish brogue. "Now I hear that he is nothing more than a Papist-loving gunrunner, aided by a Jewish floozie!"

Decades later, Ian Paisley would recount how his words on the occasion of the Mulvaney arrest were heard far and wide—in Australia, even—and became the slogan for a great global communications network.

"I am not a floozie," my mother declared.

"Ida!" everyone—except the Northern Irish Secretary—said in unison. "He's not talking about *you!*"

Clutching Queen Asta, my mother dug into her psychedelic carry-on and pulled out *Exodus,* her airplane book.

"A *homicidal* Jewish floozie!" Paisley added.

Who, I wondered, had told him about my kindergarten teacher?

My mother shook her finger at Paisley and waved Leon Uris in his face. "People who have an ancient history in a land should run it."

I put my head in my hands. My mother was shouting IRA rhetoric at Ian Paisley.

The room went silent. Like the start of a funeral.

Then from out of nowhere came a tap-tap-tap.

The old bear was tapping his walking stick. Thoughtfully.

I saw my mother examining his face. She took a breath.

"As a Protestant..." my mother said.

Mouths around the room dropped.

"As a Protestant *Jew...*"

Paisley stopped tapping and looked at my mother with genuine interest. "I understand what the good Unionists of Northern Ireland are suffering...."

Where had she learned to flip-flop on the big issues like this? From watching American presidential elections on television? From Brooklyn Democratic politics? The shul? The shtetl?

"I grew up in a place where the people all worked hard," my mother continued. "They didn't drink." She glared at me, the Real Mulvaney, Peter King, even at Mulvaney. "They held jobs and minded their own business, and they were still oppressed because of their religion!"

A small smile appeared on Ian Paisley's face.

Felshtin, a tale for all persuasions.

Slowly he bent over to pet Queen Asta. "Indeed, it was canines that helped our people win the siege of Londonderry in 1689."

Yeah, I thought, they ate them to stay alive.

Paisley raised his stick. "We, the *Protestants* of Northern Ireland," he boomed, "made sure that this land was ruled not by a Johnny-come-lately Catholic king but by those who had a *verifiable* ancient claim. The British. The least they could do is put us in charge." Paisley's voice resounded through Stormont Castle. "Instead they want us to pay taxes for dole payments to Catholic women who live like rich American television stars."

So Ronald Reagan wasn't the only one with a welfare queen.

Paisley grunted. Then, just when it seemed as if this whole ridiculous twist would be received with the dismissive reaction it deserved, my mother put her hands together, like a good churchgoer, and thanked "the saintly Protestant farmer" who had risked his life to save hers.

"Praise the Lord!" Paisley said, raising his walking stick toward the heavens.

The last time she told that story, I could have sworn the farmer was Catholic.

"Can everyone who isn't under arrest and doesn't expect to be meet me outside?" Gary Ackerman said, quick as a wink.

In a startling surge of overconfidence, Queen Asta, my mother, Peter King, the Real Mulvaney, the Real Solicitor, Ian

Paisley, Britain's Secretary for Northern Ireland, his PR man, and my father followed Ackerman back into the ballroom.

Mulvaney and I stayed. Coconspirators again.

Codefendants, too.

The negotiators returned a half hour later to announce a settlement. We would be released as long as no one ever mentioned the planted guns.

Mulvaney and I looked into each other's eyes. We both knew the drill. Agree to anything. Write later.

"This settlement could not have been accomplished without Reverend Paisley," the PR man said, confirming, despite the old bear's complaints, that Protestant Unionists had undue influence over the British government in Northern Ireland.

"I do like it," Paisley said. "Ida and I have a lot in common. And I don't mind the homicide of the kindergarten teacher too much." He bent over to pat Queen Asta and chuckled. "Lord knows, we've got plenty of old homicides here."

Everyone nodded cautiously.

"There's only one problem!" Paisley boomed. The crowd drew closer. Slowly he raised his walking stick and pointed it at Mulvaney and me.

"They've made a mockery of everything we the good Protestant people of Northern Ireland, the rightful and righteous leaders of this province, hold sacred!" He took a breath and recovered. "They have violated the sanctity of marriage in pursuit of tawdry reporters' stories!"

"I never——" I began.

"Oh, that's easy," my mother interrupted. "They'll just get married."

"No!" I pleaded, envisioning a chuppah on the deck of Pier 92.

"Shush!" said everyone, except the British Secretary for Northern Ireland.

Gary Ackerman nodded at Paisley, who nodded back. Then the congressman hurriedly pushed us into the ballroom, downstairs, outside, down the steps, and into a commodious taxi, as if Mulvaney was a deposed Third World dictator with American protection and a large entourage.

In the backseat, Mulvaney took a sip from a bottle of gin that had materialized out of nowhere. Had Suzie planted it in the taxi? Her last act before she went on the run?

I pushed the bottle away and looked straight into his deep blue eyes.

"Do you think we can get it annulled?" I asked him.

"Probably," he said, making me the happiest woman in the world.

Forget about Mulvaney sharing this ending with anyone, including my mother. He now says the ending was all his idea and demonstrates how well he can meld history and partisan politics, even when it's not *his* partisan politics.

"It's not over yet," I say. "It may never be."

"This whole idea was my idea," he reminds me, as *the* call comes from Hollywood.

CHAPTER 40
Engagement (Short)

We were alone in our own room at the Europa, and no alarms had gone off, at least not downstairs.

By the bed he took off his jeans. They had been through a lot. But underneath them, Mulvaney was the same. "Why don't we do this together?" he asked, glancing at the running bathwater.

"Mulvaney, we do very little together," I reminded him.

He pulled my skirt down. "We better do it now before we get married."

This did not speak well for the institution.

But in the tub, it was as if the Europa Hotel had been bombed by an adamant gardener. It was as if we were falling into a great big hole full of building rubble with petals and roses with thorns and it felt fine anyway.

"Don't write about this," Mulvaney said as we dried off. "I don't think you can write sex."

"And you can?" I paused. "So what do you think really did it, Mulvaney?"

"Got me out?" he asked, drying himself with a thick white towel made from Belfast cotton. "Paisley was terrified that you might be a murderess."

"Very funny," I said. "Do you think they cared that people would write about it, as dumb as that sounds?"

"I think Paisley just wants American politicians on his side so he can keep the province the way it is," he said.

As with most stories involving love and politics, none of us was really sure why it had worked.

Mulvaney threw down his towel. "We really do have to get married."

"Why?"

"Because the PR man is coming with us to America to make sure that we do just that."

"I don't believe you."

"Look outside the room."

I wrapped myself in a towel and peeked out the door. Indeed, the PR man was sitting on his suitcase.

He blushed when he saw me. "Ever been to America?" I asked him.

"No, but I have cousins there."

I stepped back inside and closed the door. "You have a Minder," I said to Mulvaney. "I wonder if it will do any good?"

"I think I can get rid of him after the wedding."

"Are you proposing marriage?" I wanted to get this on the record.

"I am proposing that we work together to get rid of the Minder."

"I like the concept of you with a permanent Minder," I said. "It will be good for the world. You are proposing to me but you are never going to admit it."

"It will be a good story to tell in our old age," he said.

Downstairs at the Europa bar, my mother kissed Mulvaney.

"You're going to make me one of the most brutally honest women on earth," she said. "A mother-in-law!"

Queen Asta yelped.

Peter King and Gary Ackerman said they wouldn't miss our wedding for anything in the world, unless, of course, there would be no press there.

The Real Mulvaney cleared his throat, stood. "I have been authorized on behalf of my recently acquired client, a man who prefers to go by the name Leisure Suit, to offer Mulvaney-Fischkin, *and* Fischkin-Mulvaney, after their marriage of course, the Latin America Bureau of *Newsday*."

What did marriage have to do with it?

"Ah," said the Real Mulvaney. "A small point, but the employment is contingent on the marriage."

"That's illegal!" I protested.

"A small point," the Real Mulvaney reiterated. "Too much paperwork to send two unrelated reporters to a foreign location. Which reminds me, my client would have been here himself, but he is unable to leave Ronkonkoma."

Well, I had the job I wanted.

If Mulvaney still wanted to cover Belfast, he could do it from Managua. Magic-realism journalism. It worked with

Irish stories. It had worked with Colm—and with Ian Paisley. It even worked with Irish Americans.

Claire hadn't really been in Dublin, had she?

No reason to think it wouldn't work with Mulvaney-true.

My father handed out Phillies Panatelas to everyone, including my mother, Queen Asta, and me.

Gary Ackerman unpinned his white carnation and handed it to me.

"And, Barbara," my mother said, "annulments are only for Catholics."

"Mulvaney *is* Catholic," I said.

"People can change," my mother replied.

I have apologized to Mulvaney's mother for that mother-in-law crack.

"It's okay," she said. "To have only one mother-in-law joke in a book filled with so many other cheap shots is a great accomplishment."

True-true: While I wrote she cheered from backstage.

She and I have a strong alliance, even if it isn't a natural one.

Natural alliances, as we know, are not what I do best.

"Endings are a problem for you, too," she pointed out, helpfully enumerating another of my shortcomings. "But if you're writing a sequel, which of course is required if you sell a movie, you can end with the beginning."

Where is that?

"Maybe Ronkonkoma," said the Real Mulvaney.

"Maybe the wedding," corrected my mother-in-law.

This made me wonder why they themselves are not still married.

"It would be more timely to worry about us," Mulvaney scolds. "Can't get married without a ring. This book needs rings."

"I have a ring," I say.

"I don't," he replies. "And they should match."

Talk about history-making moments!

CHAPTER 41

Breaking the Glass

Mulvaney said that if he was going to buy a wedding ring, his father's bartender should be there. "He likes to be part of big events in my life."

The four of us—we had Mulvaney's Minder, too—hailed a taxi, a New York yellow taxi. It had no specified religion. But to say it was a nonsectarian vehicle would be an oversimplification, since each and every New York taxi has a different inherent prejudice.

"Tiffany!" ordered Mulvaney, amazing me yet again.

The Minder began to shake as soon we were in the Midtown Tunnel. By the time we exited he asked if he might handcuff himself to Mulvaney. In case he himself got lost.

Dan Tubridy eyed him suspiciously.

I didn't know if the clerks at Tiffany had ever sold a wedding ring to a man who was locked to a Minder. But they did not act as if this was unusual.

So the three of us examined gold bands.

Since I'm not big on ceremony, this did not bother me.

But when the clerk brought out the Tiffany Designer Version Claddagh and the Minder said it looked "shanty Irish"—American for "tinker"—Dan Tubridy punched him in the face.

Northern Ireland's only former spokesman in the ceremonial jewelry section of the Fifth Avenue Tiffany then fell headfirst onto the marble floor.

Mulvaney fell with him. But he kept his head up.

"Illegal British detention of Irish *American*!" Dan Tubridy announced.

Not again, I thought.

A slight, graying man with a jeweler's monocle around his neck appeared with a toolbox and pried Mulvaney loose.

"Damn Brits," the jeweler said. "Me da fought them in 1916."

"Great store!" I said to Mulvaney, who was now free once again.

"Don't get used to it," he replied, sounding frighteningly like a husband.

We didn't have time to send out wedding invitations, so Leisure Suit put up a notice on the bulletin board in the Ronkonkoma office. My mother offered to call all the places Mulvaney and I had been in our entire life, including the shul.

Claire helped me to buy a wedding dress on deadline.

"You're glowing, too." I said. "In love?"

"Nah, it's just that work isn't as bad as it used to be."

This worried me. If I could marry Mulvaney, even with fantasies of annulment, anything was possible.

"Oh God," I said. "You're not getting sweet on Leisure Suit!"

She shook her head. "Unlike you and Mulvaney, we'd be the imperfect screwball couple. We can't stand to be together. And we can't stand *not* to be apart."

Most marriages, I thought, are probably like *that*. Since it was the day before my wedding, I took a brief moment to consider my good fortune.

More than two hundred people, many of them cop friends of Mulvaney's whom I had never met, filled the bar and the deck at Pier 92, curiously eyeing the chuppah, made from driftwood decorated with green, orange, and white ribbons. Leonard's of Great Neck it wasn't.

Those who were invited but could not attend for political reasons—Danny Morrison, Gerry Adams, Suzie McBreeze and daughters, the Alleged Cousin, Ian Paisley, Mario Cuomo, the Xanti Zarates and their dog, Danielito Ortega Saavedra— sent regrets from their respective revolutions. Their cards, festooned with the colors of renegade flags—and one FTP sash—as well as inflammatory slogans from ancient languages—hung on the chuppah as a reminder, I guess, that we all are one.

Professor Colm McEligot sent congratulations and an invitation to meet him in Mexico City on my way to Managua. "Carlos Fuentes's bed is available," he noted.

Martin McBreeze, Suzie's husband-in-exile, came disguised

in a fake beard and told everyone that *he* was the Real Gerry Adams.

The Men Who *Did* Write *Naked Came the Stranger* came with the Men Who Didn't, along with *their* agent who hadn't been invited for political—or perhaps literary—reasons.

"Message Pending," the agent predicted, "will soon be worldwide." Books, he added, would all be replaced by the electronic version.

The agent was drunk, fantasizing, too tan, and from Los Angeles, so no one believed him, except Cousin George, who came with his current clients, Gary Ackerman and Peter King.

"If I could explain Ed Koch," Cousin George reasoned, "I can probably explain Northern Ireland."

The former Only Female Assistant Editor in Ronkonkoma—who still looked like she had slept with a lot of important men, only more so—came with Daniel Schorr.

I asked him if he had ever been best friends with Mike Royko and he refused to comment.

The grandest cocktail hour moment, though, occurred when Leisure Suit arrived in a suit but not a Leisure Suit.

Claire said it might be Armani. But to this day we do not know.

Then my father and the Real Mulvaney hurried us to the chuppah, as if we might change our minds if we had too long to think.

So we got married on Pier 92's deck, overlooking Jamaica Bay. Mulvaney wore a morning suit, which I hoped was not rented.

"I love you," Mulvaney said. "And if you ever leave me, I will have to go to Long Kesh."

"I love you, too," I replied. "You were never a bore and always a headache."

When it comes to original vows, I've heard worse.

As is customary at Jewish weddings, Mulvaney was given a glass to break with his foot.

This is supposed to symbolize the first marital you-know-what, but ours was a shot glass and wouldn't break.

"Good thing you don't get metaphors," I told Mulvaney.

"Honeymoon in Niagara Falls," he replied.

The Minder, still unshackled to the groom, said he would like that. Dan Tubridy stared him down.

"Mulvaney," I said, "if we head for Niagara Falls, you'll find a story in Buffalo."

"I am a modern man," Mulvaney protested. "The updated version. I don't write stories on my honeymoon. I just make it impossible for you to write any."

At that my mother popped a champagne cork, another skill I didn't know she had, and we drank to life's impossibilities: an enlightened criminal justice system in Northern Ireland and a long, happy marriage that was not distracting, not to me anyway.

I will end by happily reporting that

Mulvaney and I have not shared our many years of marriage with a Minder who was once a Northern Irish PR man. But how Peter King got rid of him, how he got Mulvaney's doctor's bag back, how he became not only a congressman himself but a novelist, too, and how he did indeed bring peace, or what passes for it these days, to Northern Ireland is a tale for another day. The only hint I will give you is that nobody gets anything done around here without Mulvaney's father's bartender.

Or without Mulvaney getting in the way.

Or without him telling me I am in his way.

But enough comments have been made, enough stories have been told. Particularly when it comes to our so-called protagonist.

Although my handsome, dashing husband would disagree, there is a finite amount of Mulvaney that can be tolerated in one shot.

Acknowledgments

The first fictional alter egos I met were in childhood tales told to me by my older brother, Ted Fischkin: a.k.a. *Two Gun Theodore,* the handsome, fearless Deputy Sheriff of Gruesome Gulch, an apocryphal town in the old American West that reminded me, suspiciously, of our very own shul. If I hadn't heard those stories, I wouldn't have had the nerve to tell this one.

Professor Patrick Kelly, always teacher of the year, graciously read the earliest draft. David Groff, a fine editor, saw me through the initial tough layer of revision so that this novel could be presented to publishers. Also he got it. As did Micahlyn Whitt at Bantam Dell Publishing, who lifted the manuscript out of that proverbial pile. Later, editorial assistant Kerri Buckley was smart, kind, and efficient. Deborah Dwyer did a careful, enthusiastic job copyediting.

I am grateful to Deputy Publisher Nita Taublib for her encouragement, support, and great ideas.

My editor at Bantam Dell is Senior Editor Tracy Devine, and I can't imagine that it gets any better. If *she* had a fictional alter ego—I wouldn't dare—it would be an enchanted if slightly irreverent presence that knows what you know before you do, then gently, generously, and clearly leads you to the exact spot where you had always wanted to go.

Mickey Freiberg is a terrific agent. So is Frank Weimann. They were both there from the beginning, even when I put one of them in the book.

Also at the beginning: At Gold'N Hen Productions, President Judy Henry and Dale Eldrige Kaye, who were the first to offer encouragement. Many friends listened and discussed earlier drafts with me, including Colm Allen, Carole Butler, Laura Durkin, Wendy Kaplan, Tricia Joyce, and Gale Justin.

Pete Eisner, an author and Deputy Foreign Editor of the *Washington Post,* was kind enough to advise on Basque culture, geography, history, and sensibility. Ray O'Hanlon, an author and Senior Editor of the *Irish Echo,* did likewise with the Irish. Any mistakes, though, are mine.

Robert E. Mackoul, President of Mackoul & Associates, and Deborah K. Mackoul, President of New Empire Group, gave me a quiet place to write in their insurance and financial offices, and I will always be grateful for that. They are true patrons and better friends than anyone could hope to have.

My real mother-in-law—Eileen Goodwin O'Keefe Mulvaney—passed away as this book was going to press. She taught me more than I can say about many things, including reading, writing, and teaching, and I will miss her deeply.

Patrick Mulvaney, my brother-in-law, is not in this book, and may not be in the sequel, because one should treat a great chef delicately.

Mulvaney himself—my husband—cannot be thanked enough. But never in public.

About the Author

As a journalist, BARBARA FISCHKIN covered stories in New York, Latin America, Hong Kong, Dublin, and Belfast and is the author of *Muddy Cup: A Dominican Family Comes of Age in a New America.* She lives in Long Beach, Long Island, with her husband, who continues to be Jim Mulvaney, and their two sons. She is currently at work on a sequel to **EXCLUSIVE**.